Key of Kingdoms

By: Mackenzie Hickman

ISBN: 1533644438
ISBN 13: 9781533644435
Library of Congress Control Number: **XXXXX (If applicable)**
LCCN Imprint Name: **City and State (If applicable)**

Acknowledgments

Ms. Petrilli: My push

Natalie: My inspiration

Mom and Dad: My funding

Thank you Natalie for making the outstanding cover.

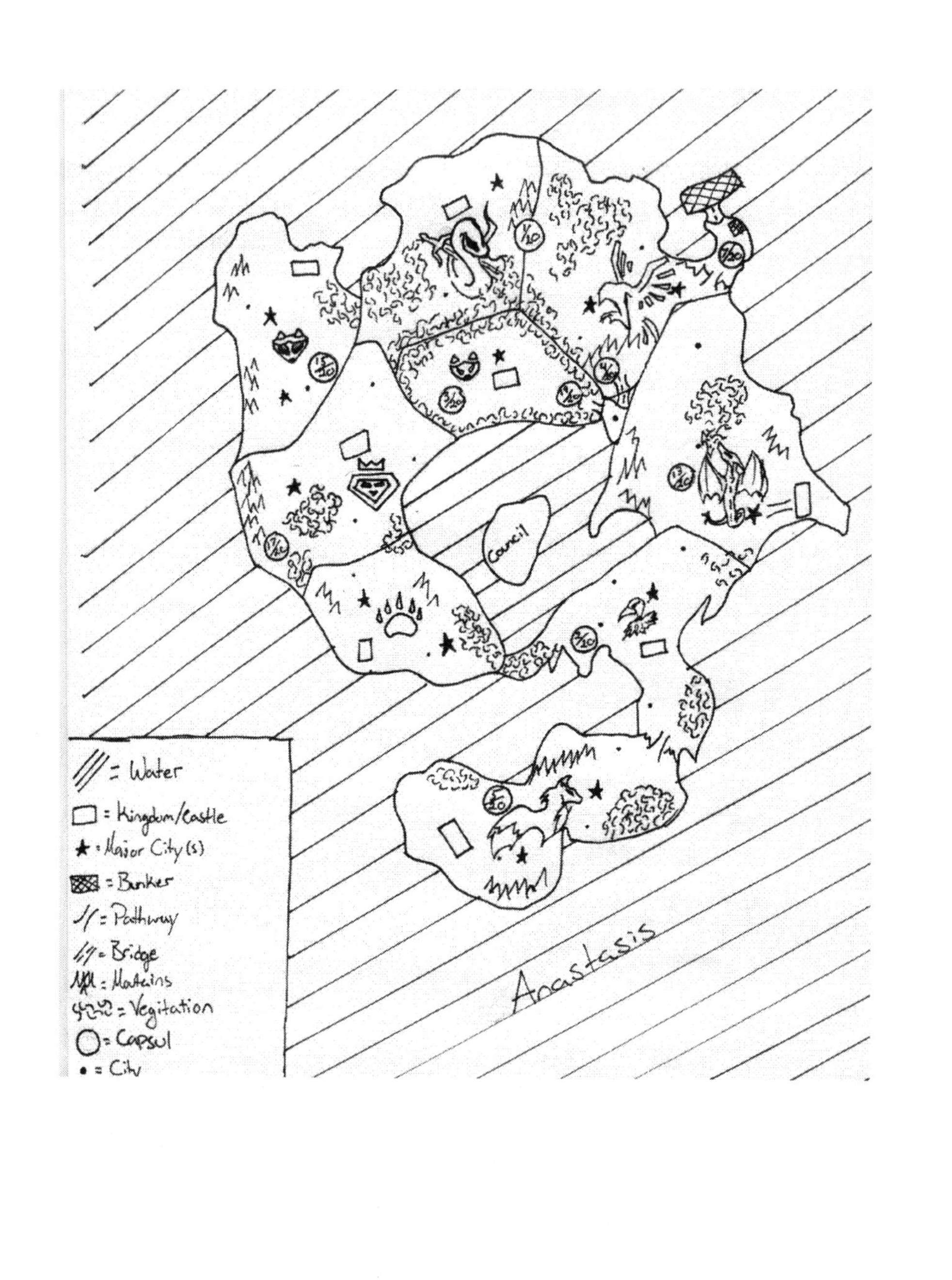

Council
= Water
= Kingdom/castle
= Major City (s)
= Bunker
= Pathway
= Bridge
= Moutains
= Vegitation
= Capsul
= City
Anastasis

Prologue

Queen Isabel

The click of her heels echoed throughout the silent throne room. With each step she took her dress slithered behind her. The light from the windows glistened and danced across the walls. Her eyes, like crystals, gleamed with intensity and kept their hold even after she had stopped in front of the balcony. Her pale, flawless hands grasped the railing as she spoke in a hard and commanding tone;

"We're going to war."

Chapter 1: *The Lie*

Year 3050

The small boy sat at a small round dining room table, his hands clasped before him as he listened to his parents tell prayer. He was not listening though, only staring at the food on his plate. He lived in a tiny home with his parents, whom he was not very fond of. He had always thought it was strange when he would see other children at school or at the local park. How they talked about their parents or clung to them when they were around. They loved their parents, yet he did not. Maybe it was the fact that they kept secrets from him, secrets that he already knew. His parents were Hispanic and he had been taught English and Spanish, although Spanish was his native language. He had always found it interesting that he was paler than his mother and father. In fact, he did not look like them at all. His parents both had dark hair and eyes while he had light brown hair and green eyes. If these people were not his parents then who was? Not that it mattered much anyway, he had a place to live and food to eat so he knew he couldn't complain.

"Kieron!" His mother called. Kieron looked up from his clasped hands into the eyes of his mother. "Chico, what are you doing? Prayer is over are you not going to eat?" Kieron only nodded and stood up. "Ay! What, are you not hungry? You're not going to eat the food I made?" She asked, her voice sharp.

"I don't feel well." Kieron responded as he pushed his chair in. He took his plate to the attached kitchen and dumped his food into the trash then set the plate in the sink. He walked back through the dining room and down the hallway to his room, the door sliding open as he approached. Once inside, he turned to the small, floating keyboard beside the door and locked it. Their house was rather small and too cramped for him, so he had asked his parents to make his room larger. They had immediately without a second thought. His room was fairly large, about the size of the dining room and kitchen combined. Kieron walked over to his circular bed that lay in the middle of the room and sat on the edge facing the only large window in the room. It was roughly half the size of his wall, red curtains pulled aside. He sighed quietly as he stared outside watching the hover cars speed by and take off onto the freeway in the sky. He watched as the boys his age played digital games outside. Every kid had what was called a Holo. It was a bracelet that, when activated, sprung out a screen in front of you. With it, you could play games with any hologram your imagination could create. You could chat with anyone face to face with it, in any providence at any time. A Holo was also a remote control for anything you had permission to link it to, such as a TV. Holo's are now what used to be laptops. Portable, miniature laptops that you could open anytime, anywhere. It was amazing to think this was how far man had gotten with technology. New medicines were created, any disease curable. Any limb able to be fully recreated. Humans lived to be 180 now, able to walk around and be proactive until 150 years of age. He had learned of the past, of how slow the world had been progressing until just a few decades ago. Kieron then looked up at the sky, how it had become a deep sea blue since the ozone layer had become halfway depleted. The governments all banded together and created a massive artificial ozone layer in the sky. Humanity was protected and now all of the governments were working as one. There were no more countries, only provinces. He watched as the fake clouds congregated and drifted apart slowly.

Kieron then stood up abruptly and closed the curtains, casting an eerie blood red shade as he plopped down on his bed. He swiped his fingers upward, facing his curved, wall-sized television. It lit up and he scrolled through the channels to the news reports. A lady in a blue dress popped up. She was talking about the new and innovative technologies still coming out. Kieron watched as pictures of a robot popped up. It did not look much like a robot, more like cyborgs you would see in very, very old movies. They were called *HEB*'s, robots that could think for themselves and listen to the buyer's needs. *HEB* was short for Humanoid Equivalent Bot. They could apparently cook, clean and even go and get groceries. One of the creators of the *HEB's* came up and he began to talk about the features of them. Kieron felt his eyelids grow heavy as he heard the scientist drone on and on about it. He was very boring to listen to and didn't look like a scientist at all. He was a large and stocky man with blonde hair and stormy gray eyes. Kieron sighed and rested his head on his arms as he began to drift off. It was then that he heard yelling, and the reason he hated his parents.

He refused to go out and make the same mistake he made when he was younger. If he went out there he would be the one who ended up getting hurt. Not emotionally, physically. His “parents” would get in fights every night, his mother saying something insensitive without thinking. His father would then retort something and his mother would begin an argument. It would happen with them alternating roles, but always the same conclusion. His mother would hit his father, who would not lay a finger on her. She would smack him, punch him and push him until he had enough. Then, he would finally snap and retaliate. Every night this happened, and every following morning they would blame him. As if he is the source of their problems. They would call him ungrateful and undeserving of their love and household. Kieron would only apologize, which would make them angrier. They would hit him in precise spots so that his clothes would hide the bruises.

He didn’t understand why until recently. It wasn’t that it was his fault, it was that they were afraid. They were afraid of losing each other, but not of losing him. So to compensate, they would give him anything he wanted and make him apart of their family for a while. They needed a family to feel complete, to feel as though they cannot separate from each other. They loved each other so much that they needed to create an artificial love for him to stay together. *Fear* is what drove them and so fear was what he hated.

Although it doesn’t matter much anymore. Kieron thought to himself as he looked to the broken picture frame of his so called "family". The cracks in the glass running through the faces of his "parents", yet his face remained untouched by the splintered glass. He got up and stretched as he heard the sudden silence in the house. He unlocked his door with the keypad and walked out into the living room, where his parents lay lifeless on the ground.

"This is what you deserve so it's okay, I hope it wasn't too painful." He muttered as he looked to the completely cleaned off plates in the dining room.

Chapter 2: *How it Began*

There was a genocide. A great war between man and machine. The machine man had created were *HEB's*. Robots that can think for themselves and had turned against their creators. A few incidents had occurred with the bots harming humans and were suspected of plotting a war. The government knew no-one would survive, so scientists created something different. Nine teens were taken and experimented on. Each was given a chip that was implanted in their head that made it so, once they reached a certain age, they stopped maturing. They were to form countries and restart society. Man needed a retry. Each were taken to the same Bunker many miles underground with food, supplies and 270 additional people. These 270 additional civilians were handpicked by the scientists. They were given only one choice; only thirty of them could be designated to a single *Dux*.

There were a group of rebels. They did not approve of the current laws and legislations that had been created in the effort of fighting back against these cyborgs. This new law decreed the removal of all books, personal and educational. They were banned in order to create military schools dedicated to training children to fight. They believed that, in order for this plan revival of the human race to succeed, there needed to be only combative education among these teenagers. The government disapproved of their protests, and sought out to disband as well as destroy this group of "terrorists". In retaliation, this group decided to make twenty capsules-similar to the Bunker in which these teens would be held in-and fill them with books they believed would be valuable. These capsules were then shipped down into the Earth and made to resurface at the same time as the Bunker. However, soon after they had succeeded these rebels were killed off.

Not long after this tragedy, the war between man and machine officially began. During the war many different types of nuclear weapons were used, which in turn scorched the Earth and made it uninhabitable for any life. The Bunker the nine teens and many civilians were stored protected them from the massive amounts of nuclear radiation. Another similar Bunker was also made. This one held livestock for meats, clothes, and other uses. The war waged for several decades. Towards the end of the war, a massive worldwide earthquake struck. This earthquake caused the continental plates to shift drastically and speed up the formation of Pangea Ultima. Pangea Ultima was now known as *Anastasis* or Resurrection. *Anastasis* was only named after the nine were signaled to leave the Bunker. This is where our story begins, in the minds of teenagers.

***

The Bunker did not allow people to age. It regularly supplied food and water. Necessities were constantly available to everyone, at any time. Above the door was a red light that seemed to never change. The Bunker constantly scanned its surroundings for changes until finally the red light-that never seemed to change-turned green and beeped three times. The bulky door let out a loud hiss and slowly swung open. The sunlight flowed in to the people inside, the natural glow filling the shelter for the first time in several hundred years.

The first to step out of the Bunker was one of the *Duces*. An average sized boy whose long, black tousled hair coiled loosely at his shoulders, and red eyes that seemed to hold live flames inside. He stepped out carefully and slowly took in his surroundings. The land was barren and deserted, large and small boulders scattered the area. The sky was a deep blue and the sun blazed above. Plants were nowhere to be seen, except some small green grass sprouts.

"The Bunker says "3834"..." Said a voice behind the fiery eyed boy.

Everyone looked to the tall boy who had spoken. His hair was dark brown and pushed back out of his face. His eyes were a captivating light orange that shown through the dark of the Bunker like lights. His appearance illustrated that he was a *Dux,* which means "leader" in Latin.

"We've been in here that long? Why do you think a war would last so long, Jaden?" A girl named Isabel asked the tall boy.

"Maybe it's wrong, or that's the year we're in... like 3050 or 2017." Jaden replied in a quiet, thoughtful tone.

"Who cares?" The fiery eyed boy stated as he walked away from the Bunker, strolling a few paces out of earshot.

"Kieron is so annoying..." muttered another average, stocky boy. He had blonde hair that shone a golden color with eyes as green as jewels. This boy's name was Ace, a cocky teen whom everyone had come to know. Ace was about to hop outside when a hand grabbed his shoulder, stopping him short.

"Hold on a moment Ace..." spoke a much taller, sturdier, dirty blonde boy whose eyes sparkled a grayish, baby blue that mimicked the oceans calmness. His name was Arsen and his appearance screamed *Dux*. He had broad shoulders and was tight jawed. Arsen stepped outside, followed by a complaining Ace.

Ace quickly turned and cupped his hands around his mouth, "Hurry up Gabs! Get out of that cramped Bunker already!"

"I'm coming, I'm coming," yelled a dark, reddish haired girl from inside the Bunker, "You're so loud." She yawned as she stepped out, hands raised above her head in a catlike stretch.

Isabel hurriedly stepped out and walked past Kieron, in front of the civilians and *Duces* that had emerged so far, "We split up the land equally. Nine territories and one No Man's Land for council meetings. Do what you all want, I'm doing what I-"

"Guys!" Hollered Ace, suddenly a little ways inland. "Look! Come look!" The others outside hurried over, followed by a few of the *Duces* that hadn't left the Bunker yet. Ace was leaned over a cylindrical chest. On each side of it was printed "Capsule 7/20".

"What is it?" Kieron questioned, gazing in wonder.

"A capsule, duh." Muttered Ace mockingly as he shuffled through the contents, earning a scowl from Kieron. He glanced up to see the vein in Kieron's neck pop. Although partly hidden, he could see the black design of a tattoo. Ace studied the design, which was drastically different from his own. Kieron suddenly put his hand over his neck and Ace's eyes quickly flicked back to the contents of the capsule as he rested his hand on his stomach where his own tattoo lay etched permanently into his skin.

"There's books? Why would there-" Jaden tried, noticing and breaking the awkward silence.

"To keep society going." Answered a stern voice coming closer to the group, "That's what they told us before we even got inside the Bunker."

Isabel turned and stared directly into the approaching girls eyes. Icy blue eyes versus a golden eerie shade of mystery. Her name was Cicely and she never spoke during the time inside the Bunker. She was shy, but knew her place in the world. The problem was that no one else knew. As she neared the group she spoke again. "That's our job, remember?"

Kieron shuffled closer to the capsule, taking one last glance before standing. "This capsule is yours now Ace, you found it, and so you keep it," He turned toward the rest of the crowd and the others exiting the Bunker, "Anyone who finds a capsule, whether it be a *Dux* or one of the civilians, it is your responsibility."

Arsen stepped forward, "No. If you are a civilian the capsule you find is immediately given to your *Dux*."

"Since each *Dux* has their own views, it is dependent on whether the *Dux* decides to keep it or let the civilian have it." Isabel countered calmly.

Arsen and Isabel stared another down a moment, a spark of difference igniting.

"So you're saying you'd let your people keep things from you?" Arsen inquired.

"No, I'm simply stating we all get to choose to rule differently and independently." Isabel countered before turning back toward the group. "We need to split up the land, equally."

Then Gabriella, the red head, spoke; "Well, does that mean we have to share?"

"Not the land you-" suddenly, Arsen was cut off. The Bunker began beeping again. Everyone turned to see the last two girls emerge from the Bunker, holding a large piece of paper.

"Is that a... map?" Ace questioned as he walked toward them.

"Yes," answered the taller of the two named Aurora, "and we've already split up the territories."

Chapter 3: *King of Confidence*

Pharaoh Ace

Suddenly, anger erupted. The air was full of tension and shock as Ace walked towards the two girls, the smaller of the two, named Kaitlyn, cowering away.

"You what?" He hissed between clenched teeth.

There was a thick silence, and no one dared to move. As Ace began to feel anger rise inside of him the earth began to shake. The small rocks on the ground dancing from the shuddering terrain. "We all negotiate what territories are our own. That is not some scrawny girls' job. We're supposed to all do it together." He asserted, his voice as sharp as a razor. Suddenly, Arsen was in front of Ace. He quickly snatched the map away, gave the girls a hard, disapproving look, and walked to the nearest boulder.

"Someone grab me a pencil from inside the capsule!" Arsen shouted. A civilian hurriedly ran over and retrieved a pencil just as the crowd of *Duces* formed a circle around Arsen. They all stood around arguing for what seemed like hours until the territories were split up and divided fairly between the *Duces*.

"What should call this place anyway?" Gabriella asked suddenly, looking over the map.

"The New World?" Ace offered. He was now completely calm and sat on a massive boulder nearby, swinging his legs like a child.

"What about *"Anastasis"*?" Kaitlyn suggested quietly. Everyone looked to her a moment and contemplated the name.

"I like it. It has a nice ring to it." Isabel said nodding. Soon all the *Dux* and civilians agreed, and decided on the name after a quick vote.

"Alright," Ace announced as he stood up on the boulder, towering over the now hushed crowd, "we split up now, and start building. The thirty civilians who chose me, come on." He gave a devilish grin. "Mine will be the best."

Chapter 4: *Fear*

Queen Isabel

Summer Beginning

Years passed after what we call "The Great Agreement". Twelve years to be exact. Every year we celebrate that accomplishment. In the two years following The Great Agreement each *Dux,* except for Ace who had discovered the one that piqued our interest, found a capsule. Mine was labeled "4/20". My name is Isabel, Queen Isabel.

I had looked through the capsule, and inside was a world history book, paper, pencils, pens and an individual book about Queen Elizabeth. The book about the queen intrigued me most, and that is what I read. I found she had been a great leader, but only so through compromise by a sort of council named "Parliament". She also made a vast agreement with her civilians. I decided to take after her, but be even better. I offered my friends-fellow *Duces*-the notion about creating an outside council. One that would not be biased and give feedback as not only an outsider, but a civilian view. They had refused.

I did, however, manage to bargain enough to have all *Duces* meet every six months as a sort of council. Now that we are all the age of twenty-eight, we have noticed our bodies have stopped growing and aging. I now notice, as I stare out the window of my bedchambers, that we have all been successful. Shortly after arriving in the Bunker and establishing my kingdoms rules, a second Bunker had appeared containing enough livestock for all nine kingdoms. Each animal was taken with a pair of the opposite gender and used to repopulate. Along with that discovery, all the *Duces* have become great and powerful with their own kingdoms in their own way. I felt a sort of pride well up inside of me that made me realize we've done it. We have restarted society and life on Earth; the next generation. This didn't last long as one of my messengers came to me.

"Your majesty! We have received word of Kieron!" He exclaimed.

"What's he done?" I asked curiously, turning toward the messenger from the window.

"We've been informed he has been preparing armed forces by one of our spies," he told, "I fear he is planning to attack and begin a war."

I stood for a moment and couldn't help but laugh a little, gaining a questioning look from my messenger. Kieron was indeed independent in how he thought, but he would never begin a war. None of us have ever even been in a war let alone know how to fight one.

"Leave him be for now," I declared as I walked past him to my throne room, "he cannot be doing what I think he is."

***

King Kieron

I've never paced more than I have in the past hour. The platform in front of my throne where I have tirelessly walked must have started to become indented. I could feel heat radiating off of my body even more than usual. I paused momentarily and glanced to the enormous columns lining the walls. Each one had a red engraving of a snake and my kingdom's flag hung midway up. I took quick, long strides around the room in order to preoccupy my mind and take in the architecture. I walked along the long red carpet that began at the entrance to the throne room and stopped at the steps to the platform that led to my large red and gold throne. I turned to face it and squinted slightly from the glimmer of the red flare of the two large fire pits on either side of it. My eyes wandered to the waterfall of lava that cascaded down behind my chair that cast a crimson glow throughout the room. I turned on my heel and walked the perimeter of the room. There were no windows so the massive chandelier that hung in the middle of the room was the only source of light besides the fire. My boots clicked against the red and black marbled floor as I walked to my original position on the platform in front of my throne. I could feel the intense, collective heat from the bonfires and the waterfall of lava now. The room was a perfect temperature for me. The consistent heat from the fire engulfing the room made it feel like I was constantly in a sauna. *I need a cup of scalding coffee to rejuvenate...* I thought to myself before I grit my teeth and remembered why I was so infuriated. I, King Kieron, finding a *spy*! In *my* kingdom! He would not speak of whom he is a spy for, so I let him go in hopes of following him back to his kingdom. Which was an excellent plan had my useless guards not lost him at the territory's edge. I cannot trust any of those glorified pigs anymore. The *others*. And now one of the *Duces* knows of my improving militia and strategy. *I wonder if they realize my plans...* Just then, two of my *Regiis*-"royal" in Latin-guards approached. I stopped pacing and turned to regard what they brought. They were carrying a man in rags.

"What? Who is he?" I demanded in disgust and glanced over the unfortunate soul.

"Lord Kieron, you told us to find any imperfects in the kingdom. We found this one roaming the streets. He has a few scars on his-"

"Kill it immediately." I replied, cutting him off and leaning closer to the man to take in his eye color. He sucked in a breath, his brown eyes glazing over in fear as he turned white as snow. "There is no room for error in this kingdom." I straightened and looked down upon this worthless man. His eyes were black, the color of imperfects. The only color eyes someone can, and should have, is light colored eyes. He was cowering and shaking with fear. *Fear.* It is a disgusting emotion. It is solely for the weak and is not welcome in my presence. Only those who are perfect may live happily in my society.

The guards then dragged the man away. I sat in my throne to ponder the effects of my decisions.

I need to obtain an ally or two to accomplish my plans... someone who can keep secrets, someone with similar views and no fear... I thought to myself.

Just then a name came to me. Someone who was easy to manipulate when spoken to right.

Gabriella.

Yes, she would be *perfect*. She has no fear.

Chapter 5: *Thinking? Bad?*

Queen Gabriella

Why is he in my throne room? I thought as I watched Ace-Pharaoh of Bear Kingdom-kneel before me. I sat as I usually did in my throne, sideways. My legs hung over the arm, crossed, as I propped my elbow on the opposite arm of the throne and my head on my hand. My throne room is at a higher temperature than most because warmer temperatures help me keep calm and think clearer. I looked around a moment at my interior designing. There were two archway entrances on both sides of the room and a single exit out to the balcony directly across the room from me. In the center of the room was a large fire pit surrounded by lavish black couches. The floor was white tile with a large black design of a dragon in the center. Lights in the floor illuminated the room with the help of the many skylights that littered the ceiling. My throne was back against the far wall and two large speakers were protruding slightly from the walls behind me. The room is very spacious and perfect for acoustics when I listened to music. My wandering eyes finally rested back on Ace, who had intruded just a few moments ago. In fact, I recalled him barging in on my personal time of listening to music.

"What do you want now?" I inquired as he stood.

"Gabriella, I have a-" The boyish ruler was cut off as I turned up my music louder with the remote hidden in my right hand. I tried to hide my smirk as I raised an eyebrow in fake confusion. He attempted to speak once more, louder this time, but I turned up my music again. I giggled to myself. The poor fool. It's his own fault for believing he could just waltz into *my* throne room and demand a proposition. He's been continuously asking for money lending, but I refused every time. He would just gamble it away anyway. However, I quickly became bored of irritating him so I decided to hear him out.

I lowered the music that I composed myself, "You may speak now, *boy*." I said holding back a snicker.

"Finally, you let-" He tried. I cranked the volume up again and let out a laugh, which earned me one of his priceless "are-you-serious" looks.

"What? I had to do it at *least* one more time." I mocked.

"Done?" He asked with his jaw clenched. He was obviously sick of the fun I was having.

"Maybe." I shrugged, now gazing past him at the beautiful scenery outside.

"As I was saying," he cleared his throat, "I have a proposal, an agreement."

"Agreement?" I repeated slowly, sitting properly now. I saw his slight smirk and frowned.

"Indeed. I know you obtained quite a fortune over the years." He replied with a smug look.

And now I've lost interest. I sighed loudly, but he didn't seem to notice. I zoned him out, pondering my own problems. Rumors have begun to be weaved throughout the kingdoms of who's the most "powerful". *It's silly really,* I mused, *it is obviously the leader who is the most well-rounded in a sense. I've come to learn I am not completely well rounded yet. Isabel has an unmatchable image while Kieron's is not as perfect as it seems. If you look hard enough you can see through the cracks in his mask. However, he continues to become better and better at hiding this. That concerns me... I don't trust him. Kaitlyn on the other hand is so perfectly pure. Like snow that has just fallen, covering the land in a blanket of white. She's an extraordinary business partner as well. Then there is Ace, the small and insignificant boy before me.*

Oh! He's beginning to notice I'm not listening. I nodded as though I was intrigued by what he was saying. He picked up his rant again in full confidence, even with sweat beads forming on his brow. *Too easy.* I thought to myself. *Now, Ace is not good at hiding his emotions, but that's what makes him dangerous. He's like a ticking time bomb all the time. What seems to intrigue me is his older brother, Arsen. I can't tell whether he's using Ace for personal gain or actually cares for him. Rumors certainly change one's perspective.*

"-And *that* is why you should give me money." He said cheekily with his fists on his hips.

I watched him a moment before pointing to my door, "How about no? Please leave before I have you escorted out." I replied mockingly.

Then I saw it, a quick glimpse of rage. The vein in his neck twitched and his jaw tightened. He stood a moment before storming out of my castle. Maybe I was a little hard on him. I chewed on the thought because we had been friends long ago, best friends. He is a very handsome man. Even when we were children Ace had always had a knack for outfits and matching clothes. He had come to me in casual clothes, including a fitted gray jacket with no undershirt made for him by his tailors that emphasized his well-built figure. He was not as heavily-built as his brother, but he was strapping in a way. His dark jeans helped to accentuate his bright green eyes. His jawline was prominent when he was talking, and I had also seen his silver wristband glittering on his left hand when he had made excessive hand movements. It was the one his mother gave to him when we were kids. I sighed quietly and snapped my fingers, causing a small flame to ignite and rest on my thumb. I gazed into the flame as I thought about our deteriorating friendship. *It's just like back then... when I had to push him away. I hope nothing like that has to happen again. It was mostly how he acted so it wasn't entirely my fault anyway.* The thoughts lingered for a moment before I realized that he had done something very strange today... *he had tried to mask his emotions, didn't he?* Ace was never capable of doing something like that. Someone is definitely pulling the strings... *Arsen.*

Chapter 6: *The Eldest*

King Arsen

I sensed him before he was even a half a mile towards my castle. I sighed quietly, *He sure is a handful... but, it will all be worth it by the time he's a little older. Maybe even in a few months...*

"Arsen!" Ace bellowed as he burst through my study doors, almost knocking them off the hinges.

"Yes?" I sighed. His temper has greatly improved, and he is getting better at hiding his rage especially.

"That wench Gab-" He attempted.

"Manners. Even if you aren't in the presence of whomever you are speaking about, no matter *where* you are, always address them justly so. You never know who is listening." I interrupted, looking into the eyes of my younger brother.

He irritably told me what had happened, I could tell in his eyes he felt a little hurt that she hadn't listened to his "wonderful" and "perfect" speech. His sparkling green eyes seemed almost drained. His hair was slightly matted with sweat from the journey back in the summer heat. I thought about what he had said, trying to find a way to quickly and surely raise his confidence without causing problems in the future.

"You've known her quite a while Ace. You two are childhood friends and maybe that's where the problem lies. It's not that you're too close or too unconnected, maybe it's that you two are just right, understand?" I asked watching his brain work.

"No." He replied, obviously lost.

I smiled a little before explaining; "Maybe she's afraid if she offers you anymore help rumors will start. You know how she feels about rumors. Having people believe you two are close would be breaking one of the three promises we all made. *No relationships beyond business partners between* Duces *or civilians."*

His eyes lit up a bit, but suddenly went out, "Does that mean she broke one of the rules?" His eyes went wide as he spoke.

"No," I furrowed my brow, "no, no. Ace, I just meant she doesn't want anyone to think that."

He looked a bit upset about that. That's a problem, a big one. Ace cannot like Gabriella. It would start so many problems and could get them both exiled. Not only would Gabriella be annoyed, and no one wants that, but so would all the other *Duces*. Gabs already doesn't like me because of her crush on me back before the war started. We were still young-thirteen years old-when she had confessed to being in love with me. I valued our friendship more, but she never took rejection well, since her parents weren't all that great of maternities. I can't help but feel her that her parents are responsible for that. She's had a problem with me ever since, and I can still feel the tension when we talk.

"Then what should I do? I don't have enough money to upgrade my army." He pouted. I stared in confusion a moment.

"Why would you need to increase your military power Ace? You know-" I tested.

"You haven't heard? Well, Isab- Queen Isabel," he corrected, "told me to inform you on Lord Kieron. He's been upgrading his military secretly for some time now. She thinks he's going to start a war."

I stood suddenly and slammed my hands on the table. "No. Do *not* draw attention to yourself. Listen to me not Isabel. She knows nothing of war and strategy. I take after King Arthur remember? War and strategy is my specialty. If you are going to invest in this do it secretly, I'd advise you to not do anything about it at all. Remember the second rule?" I taxed.

"N-never start a war no matter what differences arise." He replied, cowering slightly.

I cleared my throat, standing straight, "I'm sorry, I'm just worried about you Ace." I soothed, seeing him visibly relax. I sat slowly, running a hand through my hair. "Go back to your castle Ace, your people need you." I smiled and saw his face light up before he turned and left. I sighed and leaned back in my chair. *Kieron? Starting a war?* I thought to myself, *it's not beneath him, though he's very manipulative and that's what bothers me. He could easily recruit one of the Duces. But, who? Who would he go after?* I closed my eyes, concentrating. *Not Gabriella, she's too cautious of him...* Suddenly, it hit me. The perfect person for Kieron to manipulate. I sat up straight, rigid as the name of the perfect ally for Kieron came to me. The only *Dux* who hasn't chosen a historical sovereign yet. *Cicely.* I heard my own voice say her name aloud. The title she was well known by; *Empress* Cicely, "The Empress of Death".

Chapter 7: *Mysterious Thoughts*

Empress Cicely

"Empress Cicely". The name I chose to give myself. Years ago all the *Duces* had found a capsule. It contained many items such as; pens, pencils, paper, a world history book and an individual book on a historical leader. Some had chosen their personal titles-such as King or Queen-because of who they take after. The historical sovereign they agree with. I have found two capsules so far, and still I didn't like how each of them governed. The first capsule I found was labeled "10/20". Inside, the ruler that was talked about was named George Washington. Although his morals were great, and he ruled in the most effective and beneficial way possible. However, I didn't like how he stepped down after only a few years of ruling. He is to have said; "I would rather be on my farm then be emperor of the world." How he thought was the problem. I cannot take after such a man that would give up such immense power for his form of justice. He gave up a seat of power when his people adored him so much. He could've ruled for decades if he had just stayed put. Also, the title of "Presidency" does not suit my personal tastes. I prefer something with much more power in the name.

The second capsule was labeled "3/20". The contents were indeed the same, but the historical leader that is focused on is different. This leader was named Augustus, Emperor of Rome. Holy Rome-the Roman Empire-was an extraordinary thing to read about. The accomplishments of these people were immense in how they discovered and invented. Though their belief system is questionable, the Romans ability to conquer and battle was something to be further investigated. I enjoyed learning about these people, the Romans. However, I am not fond of Augustus. He may have been an exceptional leader, but there was something about him that reminded me of that cocky dimwit Ace. That boy has so much potential yet he wastes it on insignificant practice battles with his brother. He is always running back and forth between kingdoms and walking to all the kingdoms to ask the *Duces* to lend him money. Arsen needs to teach him to be more adult-like. Even if Ace is the youngest of all the *Duces*, he should try to be a little more responsible. However, Ace is not the only resemblance I see. Queen Isabel is also a reminder that makes my blood boil. Nevertheless, that's another story for another time. I did not choose Augustus, obviously. I gave the capsule to Jaden, since it was of no use to me anymore. Instead, I looked to the world history book.

I conversely chose the old Japanese government involving the Emperor at full power. I agree with this government system very much and I enjoy how much military power is already established. The ruler, or Emperor, is in complete control. I didn't like how the other two individual leaders functioned. Not because of what they failed or accomplished, but how they ran their empire. I believe that a just superior is only given his/her worth by how well they operate in unison with their government and the people. The government branches that George Washington took after was indeed a marvelous idea even though it was just as flawed as the Roman Empire. If a sovereign is in harmony with the government and the people I believe everything will go much smoother. This is the ideal that these two very different forms of government have in common. Even so, opinions are there to share and be recognized, but not always to be taken to heart. Such is the reason why we *Duces* decided on not only naming this new world *Anastasis,* but splitting it up into equal parts. *Anastasis* means "resurrection" in Latin. The resurrection of society is how we thought of it... well, how *Kaitlyn* thought of it. The idea of resurrecting humanity again and fixing the mistakes that had been made before. However, I have a hunch that things will not turn out how we believe they will.

I sighed quietly, snapping my fingers to signal to my servants to gather around and begin waving large fans around me. I closed my eyes momentarily as I felt the wind caress me, energy and motivation flowing back into me. My thoughts slowed and I began to think more clearly about what I should do regarding the other *Duces*, as well as what new rumors will begin to spread. As if on cue my messenger arrived. I continued to look out from my balcony over my village and its inhabitants as I leant against the banister, the wind from the fans cooling my skin gently and making my hair flutter behind me. My kingdom contains a singular village surrounded by a forest. There is only one way in and a multitude of ways out. But, it is dangerous to take leave without using the designated exit.

"Empress," He announced, bowing low, "anther poor soul has attempted to enter your forest. He was quickly exterminated though, by your-"

"Yes, I figured so." I replied, cutting him off.

"His symptoms had shown differently with the new product."

"Was he afraid?"

"Petrified."

"Excellent." I smirked. There have been many rumors floating about. Meaningless gossip has turned to chatter amongst the *Duces* about a possible war approaching. Whether these rumors are true or false I find it in my best interest to be well prepared. Especially against Isabel. One should always be weary of the self-possessed. I continued to stare outside at the wispy clouds above to the gentle sway of the trees. For some strange reason I couldn't help but think of Pharaoh Ace. "The Ace", was his nickname given to him by his people. He is well adored, but his emotions are almost certainly going to be his downfall.

"You're excellency?" Another one of my messengers broke my train of thought. I turned to him slowly and saw his eyes glaze over momentarily in fear.

"Yes? What is it?" I asked coolly, watching his reaction as he stayed on one knee.

"Pharaoh Ace has sent you a message."

Speak of the Devil.

I scoffed, "Oh has he? What does the bothersome brat want this time? Money as usual? Or has he come to boast that he's gotten a new toy from his brother?" The messenger's eyes went wide, and he looked up at me. His eyes told me everything. Ace was here. I looked up just as the boy was led in. His grin told me he had heard everything.

"*Bothersome brat* you say? That hurts Empress!" He exclaimed amused. "Ya know," he mused as he strolled in, turning in circles to look around as he got closer, "you should never speak about someone poorly behind their back." He smirked deviously as he locked eyes with me. "You never know who's listening."

***

Pharaoh Ace

The look on Cicely's face was priceless. I couldn't tell whether she was angry or embarrassed by how red her face was. She was gorgeous anyway, especially when she was blushing. She had no blemishes or scars that the eye could see. Her eyes were the color of honey, well the one I could see anyway. Her left eye was covered by an eye patch. The strap was as black as night and the patch wasn't really a patch at all. It was circular and gold with a claw emblem on the front. Three smaller coin-like objects dangled from the main eye patch. Her hair was like black velvet, shiny and smooth and it was always done up in a neat top bun except for today. It was the first time I have seen her with her hair down, her black locks being swayed by the wind from her servants fanning. She is currently wearing a black pencil dress and a gray mesh cover-up around her shoulder that fluttered from the breeze her servants created. Her curvy, but petite figure fit perfectly in the fabric of her dress. I noticed her thin arms move a bit timidly as she smoothed her dress and craned her neck a bit to look up at me even with her high heels on.

"You look beautiful even when you're angry." I told her, snickering as I ran a hand through my hair.

"I'm sorry, Pharaoh Ace. I didn't know-" She began.

"Of course you didn't, but it's alright." I shrugged, "Anyway, I have important news."

"Do you? From who?"

"Queen Isabel and my brother."

"Not interested." She huffed and turned away from me to the balcony. Her servants stopping their fans momentarily before she gave them a fierce look for them to continue.

I sighed quietly. Everyone knew Cicely and Isabel had problems with one another. It was actually a bit sad. I've heard stories that they used to be friends. The issue is that everyone has a story behind them. Before the war... before the experimentation. Telling from the stories I've heard, everyone has changed because of that. "You know, Cicely, I don't care what happened beforehand. I don't care what happened in the past between everyone. I care about right now. About staying peaceful, and Kieron could ruin everything we've strived for. I'm pretty sure we all know why he's improving his army. This could disrupt the peace we've all worked so hard for." I told.

"How does she know that?" She questioned, turning back toward me, "How did she find out what he's doing?" Her eyes gleamed with intensity and irritation.

"She said her spy saw it."

"So she has a spy in every kingdom?"

"I wouldn't know."

"She does. She's power hungry, always has been. She's probably the one improving her military!" She growled.

"I don't really care. She can think what she wants, but I for one am not letting any of these differences start something were going to regret." I stated.

"Nothing is going to get out of hand. Thank you for telling me, Ace. I appreciate it."

I watched her closely a moment before replying, "Improve your army in secret Cicely. If Kieron is actually the bad guy here it's going to be a shock even if we're ready for it. No one wants a war."

She was silent for a while. I knew her mind was racing. She turned her head away. I could only see her honey colored eye and her pursed lips as the room became darker. The sun was setting and cast a low, orange glow into the room. The lighting drastically enhanced her features, and made her eyes seem to pop from the afterglow.

"Why do you worry about me? Why do you care what I'm going to do?" She queried. I gazed into her eyes in an attempt to analyze her meaning. I could see the cogs in her mind spinning as she watched me.

"I only worry about myself." I replied after a long pause.

Another moment of silence crawled by.

"Then why come to me?" She tested.

I smiled at that and replied, "Because, Cicely," I looked directly into her eyes and shoved my fists in my pockets, "You seem so helpless." Her eyes narrowed at me and I felt her icy glare. I continued, "But, you detest help and that will most certainly hurt you more than it will help you." At that I turned and left, leaving her to ponder my words and feeling quite excited. Why? Cause I just seemed *so* cool.

Chapter 8: *Even Adoration Has Flaws*

Pharaoh Ace

I had just arrived at the border of my kingdom on my way back from Badger Kingdom, Cicely's territory. The sound of my horse's hooves going from a melodic thudding on the dirt packed road to a pleasant clack on the stone pathway. I could hear the cheers of my people as I got closer to my castle. I love the sound of the crowds cheering and yelling my name in adoration. "Pharaoh Ace". They scream it while throwing roses to me. I adore the way I am idolized constantly. I am finally able to be a big brother to someone. As I make my way to the castle I can't help but think of whether I should inform everyone or not. I should keep it in the small circle there is now, otherwise problems could occur. Big ones. I dismounted and saw a woman standing in the front row of the crowd. I caught a rose and walked over. My gaze caught hers as I gently took her hand and kissed it.

"Malady, you are gorgeous." I told her in a sultry tone as I tucked a rose in her hair. Her face became bright red and I couldn't help but smile. She was grinning from ear to ear. I pulled away and continued on my way, stopping here and there to greet children, men and women to see their smile. I love the smiles of others.

Ace sweetie, I recalled my mother telling me, *remember that you can be happy just by making others happy. But, never forget that some people can only be happy with your sorrow.* I continued to smile, even though the thought made me mull over the people I had made unhappy. As I entered my castle I walked with some of my *Regiis*, my royal guards. All the *Duces* described their royal guards with that word. As we strolled to the main steps of my throne they told me of the activities and work that needed to be done for the day. I glanced around a moment as we climbed one of the two staircases on either side that led to similar pathways to my throne. The entire throne room had a very ancient Egyptian vibe that was portrayed through the hieroglyphics, which decorated the polished sandstone walls. There was a large engraving of a bear on its hind legs behind my immense throne. My eyes wandered to the ceiling where vines and leaves cascaded down from the center and along the walls. It was good to be home again. I snapped my attention back to my guards, who were still listing off the tasks I needed to finish by today.

"That can wait till later." I sighed as I plopped down in my chair.

"But, sire-" He tried, but fell silent to my raised hand.

"No. I will think about that later. Could you fix my mud bath? I'm really tired from running around all day." I requested with a chuckle.

"Yes, Pharaoh. I will arrange it immediately. Please wait just a few moments." He bowed and turned away, walking back down the stairs.

I leaned back in my throne a moment before standing. I needed to take that mud bath and shower after before I could calm my nerves. I felt too antsy at the moment, and a nice relaxing mud fight with my soldiers would really hit the spot. I smirked at the thought. We would play a game to relieve stress, but I always won against them.

Suddenly, a soldier came and bowed slightly, "Pharaoh, your bath is ready. Your select *Regiis* are already awaiting your arrival." I got up and I was instantly behind my throne. I gently placed my hand on a marked brick of sandstone. The wall snak in with minimal pressure and a doorway was revealed by the sandstone sliding down into the floor. I felt my heart surge with excitement as I stepped through, brushing the foliage curtain aside. Sunlight glimmered down from the opening in the ceiling of an immense room. It was a naturally built cave that was the perfect holding place for an immense mud bath. Bright green trees stood tall in various corners of the room. Grass surrounded the pit of mud that was shallower on the ends and shoulder deep in the center. Giant boulders littered the entire room, and vines entangled the majority of the trees and rocks. I inhaled deeply and took in the strong scent of earth that occupied the room. I was already feeling rejuvenated.

I quickly stripped and called for my *Regiis*. Three boys and three girls emerged immediately from the connected bathroom near the entrance and both genders were dressed in bathing suits. I ran into the mud and felt the thickness of it hinder my movement. I quickly crossed and headed toward a boulder on the other side, scaling it with ease. I smiled and jumped straight into the center of the pit. As I landed I felt the mud envelope me gently, the liquid earth restoring my energy almost immediately. I wanted to stay under forever. It was cool and silky on my skin. I resurfaced suddenly with a gasp. I opened my eyes just in time to see my soldiers sprinting toward me, balls of packed mud in hand. I couldn't help but grin as I dove back under and disappeared from sight. I could hear, no *feel*, their footsteps as they kept running toward the spot I had submerged. I tunneled underneath them and suddenly jumped up from behind them. I whipped my arm in an arc in their direction. Just as I did a storm of mud pellets flew towards them. They all turned at the sudden noise, some fell backwards after being pelted and yelled "hit". The others had dove under the mud or to the side behind a boulder. I felt adrenaline rushing through my veins as I made for cover.

One of the female *Regiis* spun out behind her cover and threw a ball of mud. It was sped toward me, curving in the air. I quickly moved to the side, barely having time to dodge its deadly accuracy. We continued this until they were all exhausted and could not continue. I managed to tag all of the *Regiis* except one. She was my second in command and was the only one who had almost gotten me quite a few times. I ran a muddy hand through my hair as I made for entrance to the attached showers. My elite soldiers followed behind me sluggishly. The mud bath made my senses more heightened. I could distinctly hear their breathing and their muscles moving as they walked. Their footsteps changed from the sloshing of mud to the swishing of grass against their legs, and finally the patter of wet feet on tile. I could visualize the sweat dripping down their bodies. I was not tired in the slightest. I could continue activities in this for years if I felt like it. My thoughts were abruptly broken by ragged laughter from my elite soldiers.

"What's so funny?" I chuckled, my voice echoing in the small room. I turned my head to the side to look at them. They were all covered head to toe in mud. They all jumped, but continued laughing. I pouted, "What?"

"Sire... your trunks." One of them pointed at me, desperately trying to hold back laughter while the others erupted once again. I tilted my head in confusion before glancing down at myself. My trunks had fallen down and my bare behind was showing for all of them to see. I felt my face redden and I quickly pulled them up.

"Shut up! Why didn't you tell me sooner?!" I cried out as I ran to one of the showers. I peeked out to see them literally rolling around on the floor as they giggled uncontrollably. Even though I was incredibly embarrassed I couldn't help but smile. "Go shower. You all look terrible." I joked. They all nodded and stepped into the showers, yet I could tell they were trying not to laugh as I closed the curtain of my shower stall. *I'm glad they're all so comfortable with me. Usually civilians keep their distance. Maybe I could come up with something everyone would enjoy.* I thought to myself as the warm water from the shower cleaned my mud caked body. I noticed that my rejuvenation high began to be dulled. Maybe it was the water, or the fact that I was no longer covered in mud. Either way, I was still thinking clearer than before, but I did not have the immense perception like I had when we had first entered the bathroom. After quickly showering and drying off I strolled back into my throne room and plopped down in my chair. I was back to being well dressed once again, ready for company.

"Sire," My task attendant spoke, a clipboard and pen in hand, "shall we get to the tasks needed done?"

"No. We will begin setting a date for something special for the *Duces*, the *Regiis* and even the people! I'm thinking around late summer, or early fall." I smiled to him. "We all need a break right?"

This should be fun, I mused, *I wonder who will come and what they will all wear.* Suddenly, I thought of whom I take after as my *Regiis* put my crown on my head to prepare for a civilian visitor. King Tut. He was beloved by his people, but was he beloved by *everyone*? I certainly am not so does that make me inadequate? I clenched my jaw, but quickly shook the feeling bubbling up inside me like Arsen had told me to. *I am perfect to myself and my brother,* I reminded myself, *that's all that matters. Right?*

***

Queen Aurora

My purple and gold crown was set lightly atop my head before a civilian entered. It was a noble, dressed elegantly with a basket of fruits and warm bread that I could smell from my throne. My dress was gold with silver linings running down to the split that freed my left leg, which was crossed over my right. The silver shoulder length collar was disconnected from the top of the dress. I gazed ahead with my chin held high as my eyes wandered over my beautiful castle. It was perfect, given I was the one who designed the interior. There was a large waterfall that depicted the shape of a raccoon, which is the symbol for my territory-Raccoon Territory-behind my throne. Four massive crystal chandleries hung on each corner of the immense skylight on my ceiling. There were multiple smaller waterfalls that created a pool of water that covered the entire room except the pathway to my throne. Two *Regiis* stood at the entrance of the room and at the foot of the large staircase that led to my throne. I peered past and saw a man coming my way. *Another visitor.* I smiled as I watched him come closer and kneel at the small altar at the bottom of the steps between my *Regiis*.

"Queen Aurora, it is an honor to be in your presence." He complimented.

"I know." I smiled, "Why have you come?"

"I come bearing gifts, your majesty. I also have come to ask if you would allow me to take your hand in marriage?" He asked as he stood. I nonchalantly made the "come here" motion with my finger toward the pool of water, which caused a small stream of water to slither toward my finger. I made it coil in between my fingers and swirl around the pinky ring on my right hand.

"What have you to offer?" I asked, toying with him.

"Wealth."

"I already have unlimited wealth."

"Adoration."

"I already have unlimited adoration."

"Happiness."

I couldn't help but smile at this pitiful young man, "I am already happy." He seemed discouraged now. I thought a moment about how many suitors have step foot in my castle today. Thirty-seven so far. I have turned down every one of them.

"Will you still accept my gifts, your majesty?" He asked me.

"Of course, I thank you for them." I smiled a dazzling smile, I could see his heart skip a beat as he struggled for words and stumbled over "thank you's". However I was already bored of him. "Thank you for visiting me today. I enjoyed your company thoroughly, and you made me smile." I told him in my heart melting tone.

He looked wide-eyed at me in awe, "Of course your grace! I adore what you've done for my family and everyone's family. You are truly the best ruler." He bowed once more and set down the basket before he left. I love seeing the adoration on their faces. They fumble for words over my beauty. I closed my eyes and thought a moment about my... no, *our* new society. How the *Duces* and myself have come to change ourselves and this new world since the first day of our arrival. We have aged both physically and mentally. I am currently at the age of twenty-eight, along with the others except Ace, who is the youngest at twenty-six. But, we have all stopped aging, and we all are still as young looking as we had been when we were twenty-one.

I, however, am the most beautiful. It's only reasonable that I be the most beautiful, because I am the most exotic and I take after King Louis the IVX. I adored how he ruled in elegance and was constantly idolized. However, I don't like the name "Sun King". Only because it is misleading. The sun is indeed bright and casts light upon others. It is indeed beautiful and its glory reflects against everything. But, it is still a star.

Ordinary. I am not ordinary. I am like Earth, like nature. Everlastingly beautiful in every way whether it be in harshness or its resurgence. Even after the constant radiation done to the Earth and nature it continues to come back in an even more beautiful way.

The Sun King was indeed remarkable, however I am better. He did not care enough for his people in return for his adoration, therefore he did not receive their total and utter loyalty as I have. I opened my eyes and looked up through my skylight at the now orangey-purple night sky. The stars have not come out yet, but the moon still seemed to sparkle. It was beautiful... breathtaking. I never knew, that I could adore something like this. I never believed I could adore anything. That something else could capture my full attention. I almost felt jealous. I snickered at the thought.

I am the only perfect thing that exists now and forever.

Chapter 9: *The Inventor*

Emperor Jaden

I gazed out at the stars in the night sky. They were beautiful to watch. I was sitting outside the back of my kingdom, looking through the telescope I had made. I saw in the world history book I had gotten from the capsules that the greatest minds had used these. It even showed me the basic parts. I built one myself, and I was looking at the full moon and stars that had appeared tonight. I felt relaxed as I watched them, seeing how they sparkle and how they suddenly appear and disappear. I needed to relax before deciding whether to attend the brunch Kaitlyn had set up last minute. Everyone would be attending, well so she hoped. I am very easily rattled over things such as social gatherings so I needed to calm down. Inventing and stargazing calms me. I had begun inventing some time ago actually. Not just because I enjoy tinkering and its calming effect on me, but also because it has to be done by someone. I sighed after pulling away from the eyepiece and stared up at the sky. I felt someone come and wrap a blanket around my shoulders then set a cup of tea next to me on the small table beside me.

"Staying out late again, sire?" She asked. I took the cup and sipped it, Earl Gray Crème Black. One of my favorites because of its creamy texture is just right with a small blend of vanilla to compliment the darker taste. Erika knew everything about me and was my subordinate, my aid. We had met in the Bunker and talked for hours upon hours. I still remember it like yesterday.

It was just another late night for me. I usually spent all of my time lying in bed for hours upon hours thinking to myself in my cramped, personal dorm. The Bunker was basically a massive apartment building. The walls were thick, so it was hard to hear anything outside if the door was closed. Thankfully there was a thermostat for each room, so cold nights weren't a problem. The only problem was that there was a curfew. You could leave your designated dorm at any time, but all lights were out by ten o'clock. I couldn't see the stars and I had nothing to tinker with so I was left to my own mind. It was terrifying. Back then I could only relive my hellish nightmare of a life before the Bunker.

All I could remember was The Strays. Their acts upon me, the sadistic leader who would torture me, their hell-hounds they called dogs, and the countless fights I was thrown into replayed in my head over and over until I got up and occupied myself. The constant smell of new, *stagnant air didn't help. I had finally gotten up one night to wander to the massive kitchen that was attached to one end of the Bunker. Erika's room was right beside mine. I hadn't met her yet, but I had seen here quite often. She was, and still is, beautiful. She caught my eye immediately, but I was too timid to speak to her. I had quickly walked past her dorm because the sliding door was open. I don't know why I didn't steal a glance inside. Something told me it was wrong to do so. I navigated my way to the kitchen. The kitchen looked like any other college dormitory kitchen, except there were multiple ones interconnected. I decided to make earl gray tea and sit out there for a while for a change of scenery. As I was making the tea I heard footsteps, but I brushed It off. It was not uncommon for the residents to wander aimlessly for things to do or people to talk to. I started to turn around and bit back a scream.*

"Hi." She smiled at me. My eyes widened and I almost spilled my drink.

"Uh... Erika? H-hi?" I stuttered. I don't know how I didn't realize she was behind me. I must've been too absorbed in my thoughts.

"Have you tried putting honey in that?" She asked.

"What?"

"Honey. Have you tried putting honey in your tea?"

"Oh uh... no. Why-where did you come from?"

She only gave me a dazzling smile, "I followed you." I was taken aback by how bold she was. Followed *me?* Why? *I must have taken too long to respond because she got on her tiptoes, reached past me, and grabbed the honey from the cupboard behind me. Her body leaned lightly against mine as she did. She then quickly plucked the cup from my hand and dropped a bit in.*

"What are you-" I tried.

"Sh." She cut me off as she stirred it together with a bit of sugar and cream. "Now try it." She thrust the tea at me with another smile. I timidly took the cup from her hands and eyed the drink for a moment. "You literally just watched me put that together. What? You think I poisoned you or something?" She giggled. I felt my ears grow hot and didn't respond. I took a little sip and immediately fell in love. This was the best idea ever. It tasted so sweet, yet it was also pleasantly bitter. It was a perfect combination.

"Well?" She urged, leaning closer. I let a small smile creep onto my face and nodded to her.

"It's good." I replied.

She pouted, "Just good*?"*

*"*Really *good." She smiled at that and walked over to the counter to take a seat.*

"I guess that's as much as I'm going to get out of you, huh?" She teased. I only shook my head and walked over to sit across from her. I finally got a good look at her. Her thick brown hair tumbled down her shoulders in waves and her hazel eyes seemed to look right through me. Upon closer inspection there were green flakes in her eyes that stood out more than the brown. Her squared jaw looked more chiseled when she smiled. She was thin, but beautifully so. Her long fingers seemed to move in short, jerky motions like her personality.

"I'm sorry." I mumbled.

"Don't be sorry, dork." She giggled again. I could only stare at her with wonder. Why was this girl talking to me *of all people? Ace and Arsen were much more attractive.*

I'd expect her to go for Gabriella before she ever tried to talk to me. "You don't talk much do you?" She questioned as she rested her cheek on her upturned hand.

"I can try." I retorted.

"That's better! What's your name anyway? I see you walking around here a lot. The Bunker, I mean."

"Jaden. You probably see me a lot when I get bored. I wander around because there's nothing else to do."

"Oh, I know. The Scientists could have at least left us air hockey or something." She joked. Her smile grew wider as I chuckled.

"Air hockey? No ones played that for thousands of years!"

"Oh whatever." She dismissed my comment with a wave of her hand and laugh. From that night on we started to meet in the kitchen for tea. We would talk for hours and walk each other back to our dorms when we got too exhausted to keep up a steady conversation. Suddenly, those nights in the kitchen became late nights talking to each other in our dorms. We would switch off with each other's room and the other would walk back to their dorm if it got too late. The night I remember best was not long before the Bunker reopened. I was lying in bed, and it was almost curfew when the lights go out. I was alone for the time being. I felt myself getting trapped in my thoughts once again. I didn't even hear Erika come in at the time. All I remember was her suddenly next to me.

"I didn't even hear you come in." I told her as I kept my eyes locked on the dimly lit ceiling.

"That can't be good."

"Why not?"

I heard her turn her head to the side to look at me, "Because you never pay attention to anything when you're too engrossed in your head." She was right. I had told *her everything about me. I even told her about my time just before the Bunker. The same events that haunt me every now and then.*

"Maybe." I replied.

"No. You know it's true. What's going on in that brainy head?" She teased as she tapped my forehead. I smiled and turned my head to look at her. Our faces were close now. I felt so nervous, yet so at ease around her. I could feel her warm breath on my lips. Her breath smelled minty, as if she had just brushed her teeth.

"The usual." I shrugged lightly, "What about you? Don't you have any problems?"

"Of course not. I'm too perfect for that." Her voice dripped sarcasm.

"Oh? Is that why you came to see me?"

"Nope. It was your turn to come see me and you didn't show up. I got worried." She gently ran her fingers through my hair. I closed my eyes and smiled. She smelled so nice. She didn't have that "new" smell to her that seemed to cling to everyone in the Bunker at this point. She smelled like flowers, but it wasn't perfume. It was a faint scent. It was comforting.

"You don't have to worry about me, Erika."

"You know I do, Jaden." I sighed quietly and felt her body jolt. She let out a squeak and my eyes shot open to see what was wrong.

"What?" I asked, sitting up a bit. I realized that the lights went out. I sighed with relief. "Aw. Is someone afraid of the dark?"

"Shut up! It just took me by surprise... wipe that grin off your face!"

"It's too dark how do you know I'm grinning?"

"Because," she pinched my cheek, "I know you, Jaden." Her tone was playful. Her voice soothed me.

"Okay, okay. Maybe I was." I chuckled as I gently cupped her hand on my cheek.

"Hey." She said. Her voice seemed curious, but at the same time as if she already knew the answer.

"Hi."

"You're a Dux *aren't you?" Her question caught me off guard.*

"Yes. Why?"

"I had a feeling from the beginning. You have this air to you. It's weird I know, but I can sense it."

"Like you could sense a ghost... or a monster?"

"No!" She flicked my forehead. I could imagine her face. Her lips in a tight line, and her eyebrows scrunched together. She wasn't mad, but she wasn't playful either. I couldn't put a name to the emotion she was feeling. "You're not a monster, Jaden. I promise." I couldn't help but smile at her words. For some reason my chest burned, but in a pleasant way. From the first day we met she has become my rock. She keeps me grounded.

"Erika."

"Yes, Jaden?" She asked, standing straight now and watching me from behind.

"Why do you stay with me and put up with me? How do you? Especially with how indecisive I am?" I asked taking a sip of tea. I could hear the smile in her voice when she replied;

"Because I love you, Jaden."

Chapter 10: *Opinions*

Queen Kaitlyn

"Thank you all for joining me for brunch today. I don't get to see any of you anymore." I said with a pout as our glasses of orange juice were poured. All the *Duces* had received my letter at about ten o'clock last night for a brunch. All of them had shown up. Even Jaden despite his antisocial tendencies. They all muttered an unenthusiastic "yeah" in response.

"Well everyone," I announced, clasping my hands with a smile, "dig in and enjoy yourselves!" I sat watching as everyone picked up their fork and knife to started eating. A feast of bacon, eggs, a basket of freshly baked biscuits, hash-browns, sausage, pancakes and syrup, and lastly two pitchers of milk and orange juice were laid out. Ace had stacked his plate and was stuffing his mouth happily. As was Gabriella, but not as unpleasantly. Arsen cut a disapproving look towards the two of them before beginning to eat. Aurora and Isabel were eating daintily, while Cicely was watching Isabel with a glower as she chewed. Jaden ignored everyone and kept to himself as usual. Kieron, however, was watching everyone as I have been. We both have been eating slowly, but there is a difference. He was watching them with a different sort of fascination... almost as if he was studying them. I, on the other hand, am enjoying watching how they interact for now. Ace and Gabriella were now having a contest of who can eat the most before barfing.

"Guys..." Sighed Arsen and Isabel in unison.

"Just let them. It's not hurting anyone." Jaden said after swallowing his egg and hash brown bite.

"Meeting is coming up soon, right?" Inquired Kieron with a glance towards Isabel.

"Indeed." She responded. Bell then looked to Jaden and smiled. "Please attend this time, Jaden. I'd really appreciate it."

"I was just busy last time." He replied, continuing to eat.

"Doing what?" Ace asked between mouthfuls.

"Probably tinkering again." Declared Gabriella, her mouth full.

"How lovely." Cicely commented, her voice dripping sarcasm. Everyone paused and looked to her as she continued with a sip of her orange juice, "Everyone just adores when you chew with your mouth open and spray half-eaten food chunks everywhere."

"How about you shut your-" Gabriella attempted.

"Well I think everyone will be showing up for the next meeting, correct?" I interrupted with a pleasant smile before any nasty exchanges could be shared.

"I know I will be!" Replied Aurora enthusiastically, "I have some good ideas to offer."

"Same." muttered Jaden quietly. Arsen let out a sigh, finished with his food.

"Sometimes I wonder how I've ever become friends with any of you." Arsen reported, now finished with his chin rested on his upturned hand.

"I remember quite clearly." I told cheekily as I finished my brunch as well. I giggled at the look I received from the lot before they continued chatting. I couldn't help but smile inwardly.

This isn't how it should be. The unwanted thought entered my mind like a knife. *Why must you interfere? You're such a pain. Learn your place already.* I replied to myself. Sometimes she can be so unnecessary. I pulled myself back to the other *Duces* and their interactions with each other.

Cicely and Gabriella distrusted everyone. Arsen was not cautious enough, while Ace was too vulnerable. Too easy to manipulate. Kieron was fronting well, but his intentions were clear; he was observing everyone and their relationship ties. Jaden was too cautious and Aurora was overconfident as usual and was having silent clashes with everyone despite what she was saying. Isabel, however... I could not tell what she was thinking. My gaze caught hers momentarily. She focused on me and smiled. Yet, even then I could see no weakness in her.

Chapter 11: *Council*

The meeting was called. It had reached the sixth month of the year and that was when the *Duces* were called to meet. They all had traveled to the Atlantic-which was centrally located in *Anastasis*-where the floating building was.

The meeting room was enormous. There were two large windows on one side of the room that displayed a view of the ocean and Arsen's kingdom. Bright red curtains swayed from the calm ocean breeze that seeped through one of the cracked windows. The blinding lights in the room were embedded in the walls and part of the ceiling. Butlers and maids bustled about for the beginning of the meeting to hand out drinks to the *Duces.* All of them sat at a large round table in the center of the room, so as there was not any thoughts of inequality. Thus began the meeting as everyone got settled and chatter became silence. Isabel started the meeting by asking what problems needed to be dealt with.

"How about stricter borders?" Offered Gabriella as she cast a glare to Ace who smiled sheepishly in response.

Isabel sighed, "I don't believe that will be-"

"I agree." Kieron spoke, cutting her off.

The room went silent as Jaden spoke, "I also agree. With that new drug going around I believe it will be a good way to stop the flow of distribution." He stated.

"What should we do then? Have guards stationed along the entire border?" Arsen posed.

"No, we could have one entrance... maybe two. The rest would be a large concrete and steel walls." Aurora chimed in.

Gabriella stole a smirk and stuck her tongue out at Ace, who in turn grumbled a few things under his breath.

"Alright it's settled. Any other topics?" Isabel asked the room.

"Not everyone agreed, Isabel." Cicely said, gritting her teeth. *How come* she *approves everything?* She thought, *I thought everyone was their own leader.*

"My apologies, Cicely. What would *you* have happen?" Isabel questioned, seeming to read her mind.

"How about not everyone has to put up such silly borders?" Cicely offered, looking to Isabel with a smug look.

Isabel shrugged, "Who agrees with Cicely?" Arsen and Kaitlyn raised their hands. Arsen jabbed his elbow lightly into his brother's side. Ace's face flushed and his hand shot up a little late. The three looked to Isabel skeptically.

"What are you all afraid of? We were all friends once. We still *are* friends, right?" Arsen spoke while stealing glances with the others.

"We are. Of course we are, Arsen." Kieron commented.

"I trust all of you." Kaitlyn smiled sheepishly, "I'm a little disappointed you all wouldn't trust me... or even each other."

"Are you afraid?" Arsen asked Kieron.

"I am *not* afraid." Growled Kieron.

"Then why put up borders?"

"That's my business not yours." Kieron answered sharply.

"That doesn't make any sense. If we're all friends we should be open to each other. That goes for everyone." Arsen countered calmly at the now fuming king.

Kieron's fists were clenched under the table, jaw tensed. The room went silent with tension thick in the air. An aura of slight discomfort as the *Duces* shifted in their seats. Everyone's jaw was clenched, whether it be nervously or in anger. This did not change the fact that an opportunity had presented itself to someone. Someone who just couldn't wait to act on it.

Chapter 12: *A Buried Rival*

Empress Cicely

I was in my throne with my cheek rested on my fist as I yawned. I hadn't gotten much sleep last night because of the meeting and late night planning for new buildings in my kingdom. I looked out at the trees in the distance. No borders, no wasted money, and no problems. I am much better and much better off than that Queen Bella. She thinks she is the best, but she is not. I am. People fear me, yet adore me. That is how one should rule. Not some made up idea that hovers between democracy and monarchy.

"Empress Cicely, we found a few more bodies in the woods. What shall we do with them?" A voice rung out from the door to my throne room. It was one of my daimyo. In the government that I took after-futile Japan-there is a hierarchy that must be followed. From most to least power is the Emperor or empress, shogun, daimyo, samurai and artisans or peasants.

"Burn them. Remember; no trace can be found in the woods." I replied, not even glancing at him. I was lost in thought.

The poor daimyo just nodded and gathered his troops quickly. He was obviously terrified. He had good reason to be of course. But, the fear he felt... I could sense it. Now that I think about it fear has a distinct smell. A certain *aura* to it. Everyone who confronts me seems to reek of it. I walked to my balcony and stood a moment. There it was; that smell... that *feeling*. A stench that smelled of salt, but also of blood. I dislike fear. However, I am fair. I do not blame these people for being afraid. The woods surrounding this large village is a deliberate death trap. I heard my daimyo leave and talk to his superior who was coming with news from a certain someone.

"I could feel my heart racing! I thought she was going to kill me!" I heard the daimyo say. The shogun-his superior-chuckled.

"Well, you *should* be afraid. She's not called the "Empress of Death" for nothing!" He replied.

"Empress of Death"... I thought, *Is that what they call me?...*

***

Queen Isabel

Slam! The throne room rung out in a harsh booming sound as her fist hit the arm of her throne. Almost immediately the two small waterfalls on either side of her throne froze solid. The streams that they created also turned to ice and steam climbed the air above. The noise echoed as Queen Bella sat, glaring at the red carpet beneath her feet as though it had said something unforgivable.

"How *dare* she." The Queen snarled, "How dare she make a fool of me in that meeting! Cicely, we used to be best friends. What happened?"

She sighed as her fury subsiding. The frozen water from the two streams returned to its original liquid state. *An elegant queen does not need revenge*, she thought. *Why wouldn't she want borders... what about the drug smuggling problem that we've suddenly been having? And what about Kieron?*

Isabel thought a moment. Though the drug has indeed gotten to her kingdom, it is not an outbreak yet. She sat down in her throne. *The drugs name was called* Euphoria. *It is a hallucinogen, and I have heard rumors that there are different kinds. It's apparently extremely addictive and causes the user to feel relaxed, terrified, furious or upbeat dependent on the type. One of the many problems was that they all look identical. They are almost indistinguishable. They say it comes from a radioactive plant called the Python Plant, but that is all I know on the subject.*

Isabel was broken from thought when one of her *Regiis* arrived. She knelt before the Queen and relayed the news.

"Your majesty," she spoke, "Empress Cicely sends you a message." Isabel sat up straight, listening intently.

"She wishes to inform you all trade with her will be ceased. You shall not receive any goods from her and she shall not receive any goods from you. She also states this; "Shall you try to trade with me I will take your actions as an act of aggression and retaliate properly". That is all Your Majesty. Would you like to send a response?"

"No. Thank you." Isabel's voice was as cold as ice.

Queen Bella was shocked, infuriated and above all a little wounded from the words. Cicely was like a sister to her. Something horrible must have happened for this type of thing to occur. Yet, what had she done?

Chapter 13: *Unspoken Offers*

Queen Gabriella

I am currently lounging in my rejuvenation room, which just so happens to be my own massive personal sauna. The towel around my body was snug and my hair was in a messy bun. I have been in here for a few hours, but I have not broken out in a sweat just yet. Unbearable hot for others is the perfect temperature for me. It truly helps me to think clearer. There is so much drama lately and it's reminding me of my days before the Bunker. I hate rumors and I hate drama. As I sit here I am reminded of the strange letter I had received two days ago. It was an anonymous, and offered a very appealing idea. It reads:

Queen Gabriella,

Hello. You do not know me very well, but I know you. You see, Gabriella, we are very alike in many ways. I, for one, believe that is an asset. We desire more land and power. To be more "well-rounded". Although it would be breaking one of the three promises, *"There shall be <u>no allies</u> among the other* Duces", we would not be the first. But, no-one has broken that yet correct? I beg to differ. Do you see past Isabel's facade? Her enemies aren't clear, but those who support her are. You need only to look hard enough. It is sickening to think that she-of all the *Duces*-is breaking the very promise she helped to establish. She is planning expansion and you are the first target. Gabriella, you need an ally and I am willing to be that ally. Our team of two will grow. I am certain of it. If you want to know more send a letter to the following address, and meet me in the Meeting Hall three days after your letter is sent. You will not regret this.

-Anonymous

A very intriguing letter. I have thought about this person's offer for the past two days. I have realized that Isabel is indeed a worthy rival. However, this person is clearly looking to start a war. My assumption is that it is Jaden. He seems to have something against Isabel given his tone when he speaks to her... It's almost as if he despises her. But, war is not the answer. At least not yet.

Chapter 14: *Assumptions*

Pharaoh Ace

"You! Take the flank!" Ace yelled to his massive fleet as he pointed to the captains and bellowed orders, "You two are going to circle around to the sides! And you, come with me on the front lines." A grin crept onto his face as he set up his army. Ace slowly turned and glanced across the vast grassy plain. He could see his opponent's fleet, as they hastily moved into formation. It was an almost unbearably hot summer day, but the cloud cover and almost constant cool breeze made it tolerable.

I will destroy you. He thought to himself, laying eyes on the distant figure. Ace's armor glimmered from the sunlight. It was all gold with the chainmail showing through the insides of his elbows. The armor had a slightly bulkier left shoulder blade for defense. His boots reached to his upper thighs, which was met by the end of the upper body plating. The plating on his upper body fit snuggly and made him look a lot more muscular than he actually was. His weapon of choice was hand blades. The edges of the handle were sharpened spikes. The outer two blades stuck out parallel to his forefinger and pinky knuckle. The middle blade was larger and protruded from the center with a harsh curve at the end. The hand blades were attached to his wrists with graphene, which he had figured out how to make thanks to the textbooks in the capsules, as well as coated with rubber. The blades, however, were coated in a thick diamond layer.

"You're Majesty! We are all in order. You need only to give us the word." One of his top commanders informed.

"Good. Remember to stay on guard. We're not here to lose our lives." Ace responded, "Oh, and don't fight *him*." He pointed an armored finger at the distant figure at the front lines, whose stark red cape was being blown by the wind, "He's mine."

"Of course, sire!" the commander saluted and marched to his legion of soldiers to tell. Ace felt his hair stir from the sudden gust of wind and smirked devilishly. *Ready then, eh?* He thought.

The Pharaoh raised his fist, then dropped is arm and pointed to the enemy.

"*Impetum*!" He thundered. The army behind him immediately advanced. The roar of footfalls, yelling and shouting erupting as they held their weapons high. As they rushed toward the enemy, Ace's soldiers created a path for him. The enemy soldiers ran out as well, but the figure-who could only be the captain of the impending army-stayed put. A mass of enemy soldiers swarmed around him, blotting him out of Ace's vision temporarily. Ace readied himself, focusing on his target with his blades set. He took one step forward and was suddenly on an enemy soldier. He drove his plated knee into a legionnaire's chest, sending him flying backward into his comrades. He continued on, moving at inhuman speed through the masses of warriors, and sending them airborne with each attack. However, he never touched the enemy with his blades. Before he knew it, Ace stood before the figure he had seen at a distance. He couldn't help but smirk as he watched the figure carefully.

"*Sparget*!" Ace bellowed. Every soldier, including the enemies, withdrew into a massive circle-like arena.

Arsen chuckled as he slipped off his helmet and turned to face Ace in one fluid motion. He quickly tossed it aside before he smoothly untied and released his red cape, the wind seeming to pluck it from his fingers. Arsen was dressed in his aggressive armor that consisted of silver and gold laced plates. It had large blue jewels on his chest, shoulders, midsection, forearms, thighs, knees and a singular one in the forehead area of his now discarded helmet. They were used to amplify his powers, though the one that did the most work was his helmet. He had a large shield that was almost his own height. It was white and had a lion engraved on the front with another blue jewel between its jaws. As for his sword... it was a giant claymore. His swords pommel, hilt and guard were not only massive, but also slanted upwards. The blade-which was not a blade at all-was sharper than any regular sword. Arsen was much bulkier than Ace. It would take two of his brother to make up Arsen's muscular stature. Ace remembered the time he tried on his brother's armor, which only ended up with Ace unable to wear more than half of it because it was too big for him. Especially the gloves. Arsen's baseball glove-like hands took up half of his claymore's grip. "*Impetum* and *sparget*, really?" He mocked, giving Ace a smug smirk as he inspected his giant weapon.

"Shut up. It sounds cool... '*Impetum*' and '*sparget*'; 'attack' and 'scatter' in Latin." Ace replied as he clamped down on his weapons, "How'd you even hear me say "*impetum*" anyway?"

"Did you forget my powers already?" Arsen shook his head, looking slightly disappointed.

"That's unfair, and you know it! You can't just eavesdrop with your wind elemental power!" Ace complained.

Arsen shrugged. "Then isn't it unfair to cause earthquakes under my feet? How am I supposed to converse my plans when I can't even hear myself think?"

Ace chuckled and held his weapon up, pointing it at Arsen. "Well, it doesn't matter. "All is fair in love and war", right? I *will* win this time. You'd better hope I don't accidently kill you."

"Oh really? That's cute." Arsen grinned wickedly, "Do you remember my second power, Ace?"

Ace looked confused. "Yeah its-" He was cut off suddenly by the sound of metal on metal. A surge of harsh wind erupting between them, blowing their hair back sharply. Ace barely had time to block the attack. He knew if he hadn't been pointing he would've been done for. Once the blow landed Ace had been blown backward from the force of the attack. He tumbled over himself and hit a few soldiers at the edge of the arena, taking them with him as he slid across the ground until he finally landed in a heap a few yards away. Arsen smirked and shouted to him:

"You were gonna say strength, right? Here's a hint, I didn't use my full strength for that one!"

“Wow that was dirty!” Ace called back as he got up slowly with a groan. He was now wild eyed from the sudden attack, adrenaline pumping through his veins.

Arsen ignored him. His mouth formed a tight line and his eyes narrowed, becoming almost expressionless. He was now in what Ace called his “battle mode”. He hated it when Arsen got like this. There was no use trying talking to him. Ace readied his weapons and smirked. He was suddenly airborne behind Arsen. Ace thrust his weapon toward the spot of Arsen's back, throwing his bodyweight into the blow. He was stopped short by a clanging sound. His arm being blown back by his own retaliated force. Arsen had summoned a massive amount of wind to act as a shield. Arsen then turned to face Ace, swinging his sword as he spun around. Ace grit his teeth and thrust his weapon, plunging his blades at every opening he saw. Arsen easily blocked each one with either his sword or shield. Ace kept searching, sweat beads forming on his forehead. He knew he was at a disadvantage with Arsen's immense defense. Just then he saw it, a slight opening. It was small, but with Ace's agility he reacted quickly and caught Arsen off guard.

Ace parried an oncoming offense of Arsen’s sword and swung his right foot in a roundhouse kick, landing it squarely on the inside of Arsen's wrist with enough force to bat his hand aside. Arsen lost his grip on his massive shield as his right arm jolted aside, causing the shield to slide away into the crowd. Ace quickly followed through with his kick, bringing his right foot down and digging it into the dirt. He then propelled himself into Arsen’s chest. At the same time he formed a mass of rock on his left shoulder and arm. He connected, sending Arsen hurtling backward then crashing into the ground, and tumbling over himself. Ace had disarmed his shield and overwhelmed Arsen in seconds.

Ace propelled himself, blades aimed for Arsen’s neck when he was interrupted by an immense flare of pain in his chest. He was sent backward by a two foot kick to the chest. Arsen stood and grinned.

“And you call *me* a dirty fighter?” He said with an expert forward twirl of his sword. A smug grin crept across Ace's face as he slowly got up with a cough. The blow had left him breathless, and landing on his back wasn't much help. Even though Ace had been thrown to the other side of the massive arena, he knew the blow was not serious. Arsen hasn't used his full strength, yet. Ace punched the air in front of him after getting to his feet, a large mound of hard packed dirt flew past him and hurtled toward Arsen's face instantly. In a flash Arsen chopped it in two, sending each half of the mass of earth to either side of himself. It buried itself into the ground, causing dust to manifest itself. Ace thrust his other fist this time, and sent another heap of earth tearing toward his brother only for it to be split in half again with an upward slice. Arsen was extremely fast to be able to keep up with Ace, and neither of his powers were agility.

"Shield would've come in handy right about now, huh?" Ace said arrogantly, continuing to hurtle the cannonball-like dirt. He was now using kicks along with the punches to propel them faster.

"I don't need a shield for your cheap tricks, Ace." Arsen told casually as he sliced every oncoming threat with ease. A vast amount of dust had concentrated around the two now. Arsen took advantage and ceased all the breeze he had been creating except for inside his own armor. The dirt created a smoke screen of sorts, which allowed Arsen to disappear from Ace's line of sight. The air was a lot thicker for Ace now, and it was suddenly much hotter than it had been. He began to sweat, but just as suddenly as the heat had come there was a sudden coolness on his neck with a slight, stirring wind accompanying it. Ace felt the warm trickle of his blood come from the push of Arsen's sword.

"Watch your surroundings little brother." He said smugly before removing his blade.

Ace sighed in defeat, again, "Whatever." He grumbled, "Just make the breeze come back. It's so hot out now." Arsen chuckled and the breeze returned just as quickly as it had gone.

"By the way," Ace added, "you didn't have to cut me." Although he wiped the blood away gently-so as not to open the cut-it was already healing.

"It was in the spur of the moment." Arsen shrugged, picking up his shield and making it retract into a ring on his right hand. The ring was the shape of a lion's head. Ace watched as a knight walked over with Arsen's cape. His older brother took it with a nod of his head as he thanked the soldier.

"Are we heading home now then?" Ace asked.

"No," Arsen replied with a grunt as he sat down, "we're going to have a picnic and relax in the wonderful weather." Ace nodded his approval and sat next to Arsen.

"And, I'm going to quiz you." He quickly added with his bold smile. Ace groaned in protest, but lay back, hands behind his head.

"Fine." Ace said reluctantly.

The two brothers lay out for hours, discussing the individual and unique jobs of the *Duces.* Arsen, because of his ability to control wind, helps keep the weather on *Anastasis* alone moderate and bearable. He personally makes sure that rain comes when needed, a constant breeze is present on hot days, and makes sure that everyone is comfortable. Empress Cicely is also a wind type, so she helps make sure Arsen is not constantly drained.

Not that Arsen could be drained anyway, Ace thought to himself.

"Who is in control of blacksmithing goods, cooking and butchering meat, and providing constant heat energy for all kingdoms?"

"Kieron and Gabriella." Ace sighed, "They both help each other out and also provide heat in the winter for all families."

"Good. Now, who is in control of the water networks, hydroelectric power plants, clean water supply, and agricultural needs?" Arsen inquired.

"Queen Isabel, Queen Aurora, and Queen Kaitlyn. They are known as the *Aqua Soreres,* Water Sisters in Latin. They also contribute to healing.

"What about the-"

"The earth powers contribute to construction. It's how the kingdoms got built so quickly in the first place. We also help in rebuilding and mining in a sense. The two earth types are myself and Emperor Jaden." Ace interrupted with a smug look.

"Explain "mining in a sense"." Arsen asked.

"As in, we don't actually mine. We can manipulate the earth and get a bunch of ores that we not only need, but want. Everything from rare ores like diamonds to something as simple as coal." Ace answered, "But, I have a question, Arsen... how come Jaden has the same elemental power as me, yet he made your shield, all the *Duces* armor and weapons, found out how to create all of these everyday technologies, and his own small inventions?" He asked.

"He's talented." Arsen replied with a shrug.

"Does he know what all the strange tattoos on our bodies mean?"

"Probably."

"Is his talent like Aurora's talent for making outfits?"

Arsen shrugged, "Maybe."

"Are you rejuvenating?"

"Yes." Arsen sighed happily as the wind rustled his hair and the grass surrounding them. Ace had to admit that it was very calming, but this atmosphere had no effect on him. Arsen tended to rejuvenate outside by just being out in the grassy plains of his kingdom. He was able to rejuvenate with his own elemental without getting fatigued. It was quite the feat given that if any other *Dux* tried it they would most likely be too tired to not only use their elemental, but their secondary power as well.

"What do you think the others do for rejuvenation?" Ace pondered.

"That's private information, Ace. You know that."

"I don't understand it though... why is it like talking about going to the bathroom to some old, uptight rich woman?"

Arsen let out a deep, gruff chuckle, "I don't think that's how I'd describe it, but it's the only time we get to relax alone. The only time we can truly take a breather, ya know?"

Ace shook his head and sat up, "Then why do you hang out with me sometimes when you're rejuvenating? I mean, I know its a private thing, but how come it doesn't bother me when I play mud-ball with my *Regiis* to rejuvenate?"

"Maybe *you're* the weird one."

"Hey!" Ace pouted.

Arsen ruffled his brother's hair, who only stuck his tongue out. He sighed quietly and pulled his hand away to rest under his head as he looked to the white puffy clouds in the sky, "By the way, Ace... rumors have started."

Ace looked to Arsen dumbfounded, "What do you mean? About what?"

"Cicely ceasing trade with Isabel. You and Gabriella. There's also the growing tension between everyone." Arsen sighed happily as his hair rippled from the sudden gust of wind.

This is just great, Ace brooded as he lay back down next to his brother and closed his eyes. More *drama.*

***

Emperor Jaden

I am an inventor. What seems to be impossible, I make possible. My name is Jaden, Emperor Jaden. I have been sitting at my study desk for thirty-seven hours and forty-two minutes. I have found and taken out my chip that was implanted before the war. This orange chip sits before me as I discover countless new things. The technology is so advanced that I don't believe I could ever recreate it without the lab it was originally built in. I shall explain what I have found out. It is intriguing, yet highly disturbing.

We had been in the Bunker for 784 years. In that time the Bunker had constantly taken care of our needs while also keeping even our-the *Duces*-bodies from aging. Now, I have come to see that the Bunker was made for the exact reason of keeping the civilians safe from aging, yet our bodies stop aging when we turn twenty-eight. However, it is strange that I feel myself growing older now that is removed. Also, my memory seems to be fading with each minute that passes. My brain has adapted to the chip and has used it for storage. No human should have lived as long as anyone on *Anastasis*, and that is where the problem lies. I have received countless messages telling me that civilians reaching the age of forty-five and above, that had originally been in the Bunker, are having a lot of trouble remembering and moving like they once did. That was a simple issue to resolve. Without the chip the human brain cannot use its entire memory capacity, nor can their bodies keep a healthy physical stature for too long. These civilians were exposed to not aging for hundreds of years *without* a chip. So, as soon as they stepped outside of the Bunker their bodies continued to age. Without the chip's restoration power their bodies could not handle how long they had been alive. Not only that, they have taken in every memory of their lives before and after the Bunker. The only rational answer to this problem was to wait until they died naturally, or euthanization Nevertheless, the civilians are fine now that there are multiple new generations that will never have that problem.

After revealing this mystery I began to think what would happen if you fused two chips. I had conducted an experiment-the one I am currently in the middle of-and discovered that I have eight "slots", so to speak, for chips not including the one already taken up. I have two hypotheses. The first is that the scientists were going to put more than one chip inside, but most likely ran out of time. The second-and more disturbing-idea is that they may have suspected we would take the chips of our fellow *Duces*. If one person had all of the powers of the *Duces* they would be unstoppable, but it could also cause massive amounts of brain damage to the brain or possibly cause split personalities. My eyes suddenly widened as I felt an abrupt pain spread throughout my chest, and a cough well up. My head, neck and chest suddenly felt like they were being ripped apart. I brought my hand to my face and coughed violently. My hand came away red.

"Erika!" I croaked.

She was suddenly in the doorway. Her eyes were side with concern, "What is it? What's wrong?"

I checked the time once more and then handed her my chip. "Put it back... quickly please." She did as I told her. The pain subsided as suddenly as it had come.

"What was wrong?" She asked.

"The chip, if removed, will cause our brains to begin deteriorating after three days." I replied.

She sighed in relief, "Are you going to take it out again?"

"There is no need anymore. I have found out what they are for and how they were made."

My next concern was the tattoos. *Why had they been etched into our skin in different locations?* I thought to myself as I looked to my wrist on my right hand where a tattoo had been inscribed. Is it an Achilles heel sort of marking? Or does it have deeper meaning?

"I found something you might want to see, Jaden." Erika told me, handing over the world history book. I looked at the open page and gaped.

"Those are... it has my marking." I said in awe.

"Jaden... Don't you have to go-"

"Yes I do," I replied cutting her off, marking the page, "I'll get going then. It's already that time of the day, huh?"

"Yes it is. It always helps you think clearer in the morning."

"Indeed. Mind accompanying me this time around?" I offered my hand to her with a smile.

"But... doesn't it benefit you more if you're alone?"

"We both know how I get too absorbed into my own head when I'm alone."

She slowly fit her hand into my own, "Yes, I know. I'll always be here to pull you out." I looked into her eyes a moment as I ran my thumb delicately over hers. I quickly turned my head away and started walking with her along the pathway to the natural rainforest nearby. It was my rejuvenation spot. Something about being absorbed in nature calms me and allows my chip abilities to enhance tenfold. I wanted to do more research on it, but it was the type of experiment that needed to be done on someone other than myself. I was certain that no *Dux* would help out so I had been putting it off for quite some time.

"Jaden?"

"Yes?" My attention snapped back to her. She only giggled and looked forward as we approached the entrance to the rainforest. *How did we get here so fast?* I thought to myself.

"See? I'll always be here to pull you back out."

***

Queen Gabriella

Gabriella walked into the dimly lit Meeting Hall. The windows surrounding it were separated and each one drawn closed, except for one that let the moonlight spill in so late in the day. She looked around and caught a glimpse of the shape of a figure on the other side of the large circular table. The person standing on the other side was obviously male, and she immediately knew who it was. His eyes shown through the dark clearly.

"I knew it was you." She told, standing tall and squaring her shoulders. She let her hand brush the handle of her hidden knife for reassurance.

A thick and foreboding laugh rung out, and made her tense. "Always so smart. That's what makes you perfect. Shall I explain everything now?"

"Um, yeah. *Obviously*, you psycho." Gabriella retorted, receiving a mischievous smirk.

The figure stepped out from the shadows with his hands behind his back in a gold and black jacket. He had a gold and silver fitted waistcoat and his dress pants were also a dull gold color. He was not exactly muscular, but there was definition to his body. His heeled dress shoes had an intricate gold design on the toe that matched his outfit, and made it so he was now a few inches taller than Gabriella. The light from one of the windows peered through the slight separation in the curtain, revealing the face of the man in front of Gabriella. His expression was one of pure enjoyment and a diseased mind that sent chills through her. His eyes were a red and orange color of fire that seemed to peer into her every thought, leaving her feeling invaded.

"Well, well, well. I commend you for coming. I honestly didn't think you'd show... I thought you'd be too afraid." He said slyly.

"No, Kieron." Her words dripped acid as she spoke, "I was actually intrigued in who in their right mind would want to start a war. Seems like it was someone who wasn't even in their right mind."

"Tell me, before I begin to explain, who did you think sent you that letter?" He asked, smirking.

Gabriella shrugged, "To be honest I thought it was either Jaden or Cicely."

"Good guesses, very good. Nevertheless, allow me to explain." He stated as he took a chair and sat before motioning for her to take a seat. She hesitated momentarily before sitting and found it increasingly difficult to maintain eye contact with him. "As I had stated in the letter, you are in desperate need of an ally should I begin stage three without you. Isabel will seek to have any possible allies of mine cut off immediately at that time and well, darling... you're a possible ally."

"Whoa, hold on. Why am *I* a possible ally? To *you* of all people?" asked Gabriella.

"Because you take after Napoleon. Anyway, besides that I wanted to explain why you are a perfect ally. You fear nothing, and we desire the same thing. A difference." Whether Gabriella liked it or not she was interested. She sat watching him curiously, but cautiously.

"So why would anyone, especially Isabel, think that I'm a possible ally to a freak like you?"

Kieron brushed off the insult and continued, "Isabel could easily see that who you take after and who I take after desire similar things. They think the same way just like we do. That's why we would be a great team and why she would instantly suspect you. Plus, you know what the map looks like." He gestured toward the large map of *Anastasis* hanging on the wall by them, "She could *crush* you with her pinky if she wanted. That's why you need help. You *need* me."

"I don't *need* anyone. Just because the leaders we take after are similar doesn't mean we are. She knows me." She replied with a glare.

"I hate to be the bearer of bad news, but are you *sure* she'd believe you? After you met me for this meeting that's already enough evidence that you could be sympathizing with my cause. You really do need me."

"I can handle myself. I'm very capable you know." She growled.

He smirked in amusement, "Oh are you? Is that why you so desperately want to be friends with Isabel and prove yourself to her? Because you're *capable*? Or is it because you're *scared*?"

"I am not scared!" She said angrily.

"Good. Then you'll join me in the road to making *Anastasis* a better place?" He inquired.

"Absolutely not. I'm not helping you create drama. War is not the answer Kieron, and you know it. You just want this whole place to yourself don't you?"

That earned an angry scowl from Kieron. "How dare you. I offered you a place on the winning side and you treat me like this?" His scowl turned into a malicious grin. "That's why you're perfect. I'll offer you once more, would you like to join the side that will win? That's going to make you the best and strongest *Dux* of all? The side that will make a relevant difference and will change *Anastasis* for the better *forever*?"

She watched him, and took in every word he spoke. He is insane. A madman. He's going to start a war that will be catastrophic. She knew what she had to do. With one swift motion she flicked her wrist and sent her hidden blade flying towards his neck. It cut through the air with a sharp *whoosh*, yet it was stopped almost immediately just before the tip touched his collar. His hands were still at his sides, resting on the arms of the chair he was in. The blade was *floating* in midair! He looked at her with his blazing eyes. He smirked, and she felt a jolt of anxiety rush through her. He had not only stopped her blade, but he had sent it flying back at her at twice the speed. She felt the icy metal touch her skin and the sharp sting that followed. She did not move. She only glowered at him like a cornered animal.

"That is what I mean by "no fear", Queen Gabriella." He told her nonchalantly, "But, you hardly understand... I'm *very* unforgiving." The dagger began to draw blood as the pressured increased. She felt a lump form in her throat as her chest began to tighten. "You have lost your chance, though there would be no point in killing you here."

He stated as he stood and walked to the door, he turned his head and looked to her in a sideways glance. She still did not move. She knew if she did he would kill her instantly.

"However, you will be a *very* admirable opponent... I look forward to killing you. I'll make that a promise." He left then, and the blade dropped as the door shut behind him. Gabriella took a deep, ragged breath as she tried to fight the urge to hyperventilate as his words sunk in.

Kieron is going to kill me. He's going to kill everyone who disagrees with him. He's going to start a war.

Chapter 15: *Party Secrets*

Pharaoh Ace

The music echoing throughout the ballroom of Ace's castle was a classical piece. He didn't know who it was by, but he did know that it seemed fitting for a fancy party. Only his own people had shown up so far. He had planned this party ahead of time during early summer, and had been preparing for it ever since. He himself was wearing a hunter green jacket with a white and dark olive green waistcoat. He straightened his matching green bowtie as he cleared his throat, walking out of the ballroom. His shoes were brown and his hair was styled up in a much more interesting, way than usual. Ace was also wearing his silver bracelet off to show. Suddenly, the doors opened and his first guest arrived.

"Arsen! No surprise you're the first of the *Duces* to come." Ace said with a smile.

Arsen nodded and gave a smile in return, "I couldn't pass up my brother's party now could I? I like your suit by the way." Arsen wore a silver satin dress jacket, matching tie and black waistcoat that fit snugly against his hulkish body. His hair was styled up, as usual, and his dress shoes were black and silver to highlight the colors of his outfit. He also had a black tri-point handkerchief, which was the handkerchief that Ace had given him.

Ace nodded and walked over to give his brother a handshake, "Glad you could make it." He said as he gripped Arsen's hand firmly, holding back a yelp from his brothers tight, bone breaking grip. He then led Arsen to the ballroom. "Help yourself to the buffet." Arsen nodded and looked over the elegant ballroom. Red carpet lined the outside of the vast buffet table full of all kinds of cuisine ranging from Italian to Japanese. A giant crystal chandelier hung from the ceiling as well as what looked to be multiple speakers. The ballroom floor was marble with intricate designs of black outlines of roses. Ace's castle represented him in various ways ranging from his favorite color, green, to his favorite hobbies and style.

Ace always did have a knack for decoration and clearly showed the best of his skills with this party. He had disappeared from Arsen's side now to go and wait for guests. Another guest had appeared a few minutes after Arsen's arrival. Isabel, who was accompanied by Jaden, approached the doors. The two were deep in conversation as they walked in, but they were not touching. Jaden's hands were firmly shoved into his pockets. What amazed Ace was that even though Jaden was slouched forward and Isabel was in heels, he was still almost a full head taller than her. Jaden was wearing a classy navy blue blazer that resembled a shorter overcoat of sorts. It seemed to be just a little baggy on his slender frame. Underneath his blazer was a lighter blue waistcoat and white undershirt. His dress pants were black as well as his shoes and he had a matching blue and black striped ascot. His suit was matching Isabel's in a way, since she was wearing a royal blue strapless dress with multiple white buttons that gave a sort of wavy look to it. The dress fit her slender figure perfectly. She was not exactly frail looking, but she did not have any obnoxious curves like Aurora. Her hair was curled and done up in crown braid. She also wore a gold necklace and light blue elbow length gloves that only revealed her ring fingers. Her gold sapphire ring seemed to glitter on her left hand as she tucked a strand of hair behind her ear. *Her* Item... Ace's eyes flicked to her left shoulder, where the bottom sliver of her tattoo showed for a brief moment before her hand returned to her side. *And her tattoo.*

"Good evening Queen Isabel and Emperor Jaden. I'm glad you could make it." Said Ace.

"Good evening to you as well. But, I believe I've told you multiple times to just entitle me as Isabel or Bell, Ace." Isabel replied with a sigh. She gave him a gentle smile as though she were an older sister.

Jaden nodded in agreement, "Just 'Jaden' is fine too." He muttered quietly.

"Fine. Just thought I'd be formal." Ace pouted, "Anyway, enjoy yourselves! My *Regiis* will guide you to the ballroom and you may explore the castle as you please." Ace stepped aside to allow them through, his *Regiis* accompanying them. Isabel and Jaden walked to the ballroom and greeted Arsen. Ace had quickly tailed them to see how they would interact with his elder brother. The three engaged in conversation immediately and they were given drinks by one of the many waiters. Jaden had one hand in his pocket and a glass of champagne in the other while Isabel held her glass with the stem in between her middle and ring finger. Arsen, however, had no drink in hand, and his hands were stuck firmly in his pockets as he talked to the two before him. Ace couldn't help but smile to himself before walking back to his position in front of the entrance to his castle.

The two large oak doors of the front of Ace's palace were opened yet again to reveal another guest for the night. Ace's smile was turned into a goggled look as he laid eyes on the new arrival. His heart skipped a beat, and he felt a lump in his throat.

"Wipe that dumb look off of your face, Ace." Gabriella told as she sauntered through the doors, catching the attention of every civilian and guard in the immediate area. Ace could faintly hear the complimenting gossip about Gabriella. She had behind her four large, hefty *Regiis* in black and white suit and ties. They gave Ace a scowling look as he gawked at their leader. Gabriella was wearing a black and white tight-fitting dress with an open back. It had a complex gold design down her left side and the fabric hugged her curves more than any of the other women he had seen so far. She also had a gold and silver necklace that complimented her gray and jeweled eye makeup. Her dark reddish hair seemed to make her eyes pop more as she slowly raised her head to make eye contact with him. Her lips were a glowing peach color that captured his attention first more than anything. The second thing that had caught Ace's initial attention was Gabriella's *Item*. It was a black dragon earring on her right ear. He was broken from his reverie from Gabriella snapping in his face.

"Hey. Are you gonna greet me or not? Also, what kind of music do you have playing?" She asked in an annoyed tone.

"Oh, sorry." He stammered, gaining some color to his face, "Good evening, Gabriella. You look absolutely stunning... like you look so ho-" he was stopped short from the *Regiis* letting out a protective growl. "-I mean, just gorgeous." He finished with a cheeky smile to the guards.

She was giving him a smirk that gave him chills. "Thanks." She said shortly as she walked past. "I'll help liven up this party. By the way, Classical is *so* 1,300 years ago." She said with a snicker. Her *Regiis* passed by and one plucked the drink from his hand before following their leader. Ace sighed and ran a hand through his hair as he took a deep breath. Gabriella walked over and greeted the current party of *Duces* before walking to where the music player was. In a few minutes the entire castle was booming with music that was definitely not classical. Ace remembered the song as the one Gabs had teased him with a while ago.

Ace sighed and waited patiently for the next guest. He remembered Arsen's lecture about how if you are going to have a party you should greet every guest coming. But, Arsen had *also* told him to enjoy himself at his own party. Ace looked up as the doors opened. Moonlight poured in and around the figure that stepped inside.

An angel... He thought. Then he realized just who it was in the massive strapless purple and gold frilled dress. Despite its massiveness Ace could still outline her outrageous figure despite her large dress. Aurora was not much shorter than Ace without heels, so her height with them made her more intimidating. She was indeed gorgeous, but a bit overdone in Ace's opinion. She had on one of her many purple and gold crowns and her makeup was done up more extravagantly than usual.

Never mind, he thought, *just Aurora.* She stepped in, surrounded by a dozen or so *Regiis*. They were all in purple and white suit and tie outfits that seemed to not only match Aurora's dress, earrings, makeup and other unnecessary accessories, but make her even more luminous. Ace held back an annoyed groan and plastered on a fake smile.

"Queen Aurora!" He exclaimed with fake enthusiasm, "So amazing you could take time out of your evening to come and join this party."

"I know darling," she replied with her nose in the air, "I almost decided not to come, but I had just designed this new dress. How do you like it?" She asked, flipping her unique new hairstyle to the side. Her long, bright purple and white nails glittered obnoxiously against the lights in the castle, "Don't I look sumptuous?"

"It's something all right..." He muttered. Ace immediately regretted it when he received one of the deadliest looks he had ever seen. It even topped Gabriella's angry look. If looks could kill he was sure this one was the kind that tortured you before you died. "I-uh mean of course you look incomparable! I was absolutely stunned when you came in... In fact, I actually thought an angel had walked in." He declared. That did the trick. The angered look was wiped from Aurora's face, but her *Regiis* didn't seem to buy it. He wasn't *really* lying. He *had* thought it was something else, and he did believe something unordinary had walked through his doors. Ace smiled a bold smile before the over-exaggerated Queen thrust her hand in his face. Aurora's full gold pinky ring glittered from the mix of moonlight and indoor lights.

That must be her Item... Ace thought. She cleared her throat loudly as she kept her hand held out. Ace quickly caught on and took her hand gently before kissing the top. "Welcome, your Majesty." He greeted. Aurora seemed pleased enough and walked by. All the while Ace was given countless dirty looks by her many large and burly bouncer-like *Regiis*. As she walked by he almost choked on the smell of her stifling perfume. It was then that Ace realized Queen Kaitlyn had been behind Aurora the entire time.

"Q-queen Kaitlyn," He stammered, embarrassed he hadn't welcomed her properly. In fact, he hadn't even noticed her presence at all.

She held up a hand and gave a heartwarming smile, "Don't worry. I know Aurora is quite a handful so don't apologize. I'm glad I could make it in time." Ace nodded and gave her a proper welcoming.

"I'm glad you could make it as well. You look stunning by the way." He said with a charming smile. Kaitlyn was wearing a single strap slim yellow dress with three silver stripes on the upper body. She was curvy as well, but in a more modest way. She had matching silver earrings and bracelets along with a silver bow on her right side. She also had matching silver mesh elbow length gloves. However, the one on the right captured his attention. He thought he could see a black tattoo underneath and the fact that it looked to have *claws*. Ace had been so caught up trying to decipher what the design of the tattoo was that he hadn't caught the quick sneer Kaitlyn gave.

"Thank you. You know, you're as handsome as ever in that suit." She complimented. She walked past, and it was then that Ace had caught a look in her eyes. He thought he imagined the small mischievous grin as she entered. Only after Kaitlyn had passed by did he notice the three politely smiling *Regiis* that accompanied her. How did he not notice them earlier? They were not as burly as Gabriella and Aurora's *Regiis,* but they still stood out enough. He brushed off the abnormality and looked to his final two guests. Both of them seemed to be matching, and they were talking. Ace couldn't quite hear what exactly they were speaking about, but it made him uneasy. What sent shivers down his back was that the two seemed so... *friendly*. Kieron and Cicely approached, arm in arm, to the castle doors. Kieron wore a custom made burgundy jacket with a white handkerchief in citadel style. The bespoke jacket had an intricate design of red and black that lined just above the singular button on his waist. His outfit was snug against his broad shoulders and fit him perfectly. Kieron was eye level with Ace, which made him feel uneasy for some reason. He wore only a black undershirt and silver tie and his dress pants were black with a white belt and his shoes were black and velvet red. Ace caught a glimpse of something on the right side of Kieron's neck that looked like a tattoo. But, Kieron adjusted his collar, and concealed the tattoo before Ace could determine what it was. He seemed confident as he approached alongside Cicely, and his eyes just intensified his striking look altogether. He matched Cicely's dark brownish-black dress. It was frilled at the top to her mid waist and the rest of the dress came down to her knees. Her makeup was done up, yet not as obnoxiously as Aurora's had been. Cicely had a large brown flower that sat on the right side of her head. It also paid tribute to her hair that was done up in a neat bun. She also had black and white stiletto heels on, as well as small hoop earrings to match.

"Glad you guys could make it, you both look awfully chummy." Ace said awkwardly as they approached.

"Kieron was just being a gentleman, Ace. Something you've probably never learned." Cicely said, almost defensively.

"Now, now, Cicely. Why don't you give the boy a break? He probably hasn't had a chance to partake in his own party yet. He has been a gentleman so far with greeting guests." Kieron corrected. He smoothly took his arm back from Cicely's to offer a handshake to Ace. Ace gave a smug smile to the unkind Empress and shook Kieron's hand.

"You both enjoy yourselves then." Ace stated. Suddenly, he felt a sharp burning pain on his hand and ripped it free of Kieron's. "Ow!" He cried.

"Well, thanks for greeting us." Said Kieron. Cicely and the snake shared criminal smile as they walked past Ace, ignoring his momentary pain. The Empress lightly shoved him to the side as she passed by. Ace looked down at his hand that was now a dark red color. It almost looked as if he had gotten burned from a hot pan.

Did he burn *me?* Ace thought to himself in bewilderment. He thought a moment at how distrusting Kieron really is, and how he seemed so cold hearted. Ace shook his head. Those were just rumors, and Arsen had told him that you should believe nothing you hear and only half of what you see. The music had changed multiple times now since Gabriella had arrived. The castle was booming with life. It seemed as if almost everyone in *Anastasis* was in his castle. Ace soon lost himself in thought. He was unable to help himself as he tapped his foot along to the beat of the song now playing. His mind began wandering and-for some reason-paused on the thought of Gabriella. She had looked dazzling her dress. He hadn't even thought she would come. He couldn't wrap his head around these strange feelings for someone who was so mean to him. She always teased him and acted as if she hated him. But, if she hated him why would she come? He was so caught up in thought that he didn't hear the loud clicking of heels approaching from behind.

"Aren't you going to join the party, stupid?" Gabriella's voice rang out, causing Ace jump and spin around quickly

"Oh, uh yeah. I'm coming." He said and began walking with her, "Wait, did you just call me stupid?"

"Got a problem with it?" She asked looking to him with a raised eyebrow.

"I just thought you'd call me something a little harsher than 'stupid'." He replied with a chuckle.

She shoved him lightly as they walked, "Fine. I'll refer to you as an 'idiotic child' from now on." She retorted with a shrug.

"Hey!" He pouted, "I'm *not* a child."

"So, just an idiot?"

"I'm cool with that." He shrugged, earning a laugh from her. He walked into the ballroom with her and felt the vibrations of the music's intensity for the first time that night. His chest was booming with it and his head began to pound.

"The music is kinda-" He tried.

"What?!" Gabriella yelled, interrupting him with a goofy smile.

"It's kind of loud don't you think?" He shouted back over the music.

"That's the point!" She hollered in response before taking his hand and dragging him into the crowd.

***

Isabel was still with Arsen and Jaden continuing their calm discussion, when suddenly loud booming music erupted. She jumped in surprise and looked around wildly. Arsen had somehow managed to stay still. He didn't seem fazed in the slightest.

"Calm down, Bell." Jaden told in his usual quiet tone against Isabel's ear.

Arsen nodded and closed his eyes a moment. Suddenly, the sound seemed to be muffled and less loud.

"I had a feeling Gabriella would do something when I saw her heading to the DJ stand." Arsen informed in a normal tone, "I was a little late manifesting my power, but it should be alright for you two now."

"You've used your wind power to redirect the sound waves in a certain manner so we could hear each other properly, yet the music became muffled and less obnoxious." Jaden said in fascination.

Arsen shrugged and smiled, "Not that big of a deal, really." Isabel cast an irritable scowl to Gabriella, who in turn gave her a mocking smile. She began yelling and shaking her free hand at her.

"You are such a *hooligan*! Why don't you learn to enjoy a quiet conversation and music for once?! How come *you* of all people are deciding the music choice anyway?!" Isabel cried at the teenage mind inside a twenty-eight year olds body on the DJ stage. To add fuel to the fire Gabriella stuck her tongue out, which made Isabel go full force into her lecturing.

"Bell, don't mind her. We have important things to discuss anyway." Jaden said quietly.

"Yes, like the whole Kieron deal. The rumors that had spread about him upgrading his army, and how he truly treats his people... It's like he's a *dictator.*" Arsen gossiped.

"I don't think Kieron is an evil man." Isabel spoke, receiving questioning looks from the two men, "I think he is just being cautious. Plus, those are just rumors regarding his treatment towards his citizens."

"Are you serious, Bell?" Jaden asked, dumbfounded at her.

"You know full well that no good comes from someone power hungry like that." Arsen told, running an agitated hand through his hair.

Isabel shrugged, "Like I had just told you; he is only cautious in my mind. Maybe he is just a little afraid. We all are in some way with these letters going about. I mean, for all we know anybody could have received them." Isabel sighed and sipped her drink, "Honestly, I thought at least you two of all people would not be so gullible regarding these rumors."

"Just remember; you don't know what goes on behind closed doors." Jaden advised.

"Well, moving on. I've been curious for a while, but who do you two take after?" Arsen questioned as he ran a hand through his hair.

"Well," Isabel said in a much calmer tone, "you all know who I take after; Queen Elizabeth of England."

"I take after the famous King Arthur. The most gallant knight and king in history." Arsen boasted sarcastically.

"Alexander the Great... maybe a little of Augustus." Jaden informed, taking a sip from his glass.

"Ace takes after-" Arsen attempted before he was interrupted by a loud voice calling to them. Kaitlyn approached with a smile as her curled blonde hair bounced as she walked. She looked dazzling in her yellow dress.

"Good evening." She greeted loudly, taking a glass of champagne off of a passing waiter's platter. Arsen quickly flicked his wrist towards the newcomer and Kaitlyn gave a confused look. "Did the music just suddenly get quieter?" She asked, looking around.

"Arsen, the grand magician for you." Arsen said with a bow and a charming smile, "Good evening, Kaitlyn"

"Evening to you as well, Kaitlyn." Isabel said in unison with Jaden. Isabel gave a welcoming smile while Jaden only nodded.

"Everyone looks so good! I'm so glad Ace invited us to his party. You know I do love hanging out with you all." Kaitlyn's smile became even wider as she spoke, "Oh, by the way, Aurora plans to make a *spectacular* show in a moment. So... just be prepared. I saw her discussing a plan with her *Regiis* before I walked in." Kaitlyn told with a roll of her sparkling green eyes.

"Oh wonderful." Isabel said sarcastically, "I'm only joking. I am so pleased that she could make it. I'm so glad that the *Duces* are attending this get-together. It looks as if Ace put a lot of work into this party."

"My favorite person." Jaden said in monotone. The three laughed briefly before continuing their chat.

"We were actually just discussing who we take after. Mind telling us who you take after?" Isabel asked.

"Queen Victoria." Kaitlyn answered, looking at the three a moment. "Isabel, you take after Queen Elizabeth right? And Jaden takes after Alexander the Great, but maybe also Augustus while Arsen over here is a fond believer in King Arthur?" Kaitlyn inquired, pointing to each as she mentioned them. The three looked bewildered at how she knew that information. She giggled before subsiding their suspicions, "I heard you three before I had walked over."

"Oh, that makes sense." Jaden and Arsen said in unison. Isabel only laughed briefly with them. *How could she have known that? There was no way she could have heard over the blaring music. Arsen had only used his elemental on her* after *we had finished talking about that.* Isabel stared at Kaitlyn a moment, but made sure she blocked any suspicious looks before shaking the thoughts from her head. *It must be the champagne.* She thought to herself, eyeing her glass

Just then Kieron arrived. He walked to the group and exchanged greetings, "Glad I could join you all." He said, looking to everyone and lingering on Kaitlyn and Isabel.

"Evening Kieron." Isabel greeted. She began to wonder what use Kieron had coming here, and just how important is it that he would arrive.

"You came with Cicely, right? Where is she?" Kaitlyn asked. Kieron seemed to snap his attention to her. He seemed suddenly very nervous, but he was trying very hard to mask his emotions. However, it was easy to spot his emotions if you looked hard enough.

"She went to go get some things from the buffet before coming over." He told, motioning toward the buffet table where Cicely stood with Gabriella, who was getting a drink at the moment. Isabel then caught a glance at Gabriella leaving the ballroom, as did Kieron. The others didn't seem to notice, but Kieron lingered a moment on Gabriella's retreating figure.

"Party is pretty nice huh?" Cicely said as she approached. She did not look in Isabel's direction for even a second. Isabel sighed quietly and watched her so-called 'rival'. It hurt her to have to come to terms that she was now Cicely's enemy when she hadn't done anything, at least to her knowledge. If she didn't know what she had done how was she supposed to apologize?

The group of six thus began chatting anew. However, Isabel seemed to be lost in her own thoughts. She wasn't paying attention to the light hearted conversation or the atmosphere. Had Cicely hated her because of what had happened in the cells? Of her own cowardice that she continued to rue to this day? *That must be it...* Isabel thought. She looked to Cicely then. She gazed at her one honey colored eye. Her other eye was covered by the eye patch she never seemed to take off. Had she always had it during the experiment?

The music suddenly stopped and was replaced with a classical piece of music that would've most likely gone with a coronation. Isabel snapped her attention to the DJ stage in confusion. On top was two burly men, each in a purple and white suit. Aurora stepped into the ballroom, a path being made just for her. Behind her, more of the large men in the same amethyst colored suits stood. She then lifted her hand and spouts of water spurted from the ground seemingly out of nowhere. They lit up with different colors as the lights in the room dimmed. A spotlight then shown on Aurora, as well as along her path.

"Hold your applause please." She announced, "I am just as honored to be here with you all as you are with me." She brought a hand to her chest as she made her way over to our group. I stole a glance at the other *Duces* and each of them had a fake half smile on to hide their uneasiness.

"A-Aurora... It's great to see you." Arsen managed with his charming smile. Aurora approached him with a smug look.

"You look absolutely dashing, Arsen. I love that color on you." She replied, holding out her hand.

Arsen took her hand and kissed the top, bowing slightly, "And you look stunning as always, Aurora."

Isabel couldn't stand how she acted around crowds. It made her sick to think that one person needed this much attention. Despite this, she truly liked Aurora. She was a very good person if you got her alone in a room with people she is comfortable with. Isabel believed it was insecurities that caused her to behave this way. *It is so sad to think just how lonely she really is,* Isabel thought to herself as she greeted Aurora. Jaden, however, refused to kiss her hand which caused a very angry Aurora to declare she wouldn't speak to him for the rest of the night. Jaden didn't really seem to care either way, he was lost in his own thoughts again. Kieron did as Arsen had and greeted her with the utmost courtesy. Kaitlyn, Isabel and Cicely followed their lead to engage Aurora into the conversation. All of them began talking, and began to delve deep into discussion when Kieron suddenly smiled. Isabel did not understand why he would smile. They were currently speaking about the drug that had infiltrated the kingdoms. Isabel continued to urge on the conversation, and caught exactly what he was smiling about. Kieron was looking out of the corner of his eye at a man and a woman. Isabel followed his line of sight and held back a gasp with a clenched jaw.

Ace and Gabriella... She thought, *What were they* thinking*? Why are they going off to the balcony* alone*?* Isabel felt her heart pick up speed and she bit her lip. This was bad. Very bad. If Kieron saw that and brought it up at the next meeting... No, if he brought it up now it would still cause major issues. Isabel would be forced to take action so as to not take sides. That was clear evidence for suspicion of breaking one of the promises. Isabel and the others had made up the three promises and decided that if any were to ever break one it could potentially ruin the respect we have established as *Duces.* So, they came to an agreement for the "punishable by death" retribution. Knowing Kieron, he will make sure that it is carried out. Dependent on what Kieron did tonight, it was sure to lead to something way bigger in the future. If he spoke out tonight, it would cause major dilemma that could *maybe* be fixed many years later. Conversely, if he decided to keep quiet and use this later on it could lead to something along the lines of a war. Just then it struck Isabel. The *real* reason Kieron had come.

"He's come to get evidence, to gain the upper hand with any kind of dirt he can on anyone he can. Especially on someone he's targeting. She thought. Unexpectedly, another voice rang out in her head. She caught her breath as it resonated, and replied to her thoughts, but she couldn't pinpoint *whose* voice it was.

That's exactly right. The voice echoed, sending shivers down her spine.

***

Gabriella had been out on the balcony with Ace for a few minutes now. She had just taken a bite of a cookie when Ace suddenly spoke.

"Why did you bring me out here?" He asked, leaning against the banister and gazing out at the moon. A slight breeze stirred his hair, and the moonlight seemed to make his jade eyes even more vibrant. He was like a lost prince. It made him actually fairly handsome. Except that it was usually ruined when he opened his mouth to say something stupid.

Gabriella shrugged, "Thought you could use some air. You've been around people all day so..." She lied. In actuality she wanted him alone. She realized she had developed something of a crush on him the past few years now. She didn't know why. He was goofy, short tempered, clumsy, obnoxious... why did she like him actually?

"Liar." He responded with a sly smile. Her eyes widened, and she swallowed hard. Had he figured it out? Maybe he wasn't as dense as she had thought, "You brought me out here to be alone so we could duel, didn't you?" He asked, turning to me.

I stand corrected. He is *that dense.* She sighed, partly in relief, and rolled her eyes.

"Yeah. Sure, Ace. I *totally* wanted to fight you out here because I'm mad you didn't get me a second cookie." Her voice dripped sarcasm.

"Oh... well then this," he quickly grabbed the half-eaten cookie from her hand and shoved it in his mouth, "would make you even angrier right?" he teased with his mouth full.

Gabriella swiftly brought her heeled foot down on his own, causing him to yelp in pain.

"Ow! What was that for?!" He exclaimed, bringing his foot up and holding it as if it would stop the pain.

"Eating my cookie." Gabriella answered with a smirk.

"You're so mean." He pouted. He let go of his foot and stood straight again. In the process of his tiny tantrum his hair had gotten messed up. She couldn't resist. Before she knew it she had stepped closer and gotten on her tiptoes. She ever so gently ran her fingers through his hair, fixing it to the way it had been. His hair felt like silk. She lingered there a moment before gradually pulling away. His face was rosy, and his green eyes seemed to pierce through her mind. They stood still for a moment. She had her head tilted upwards towards his face, and they stood close enough to each other that they could feel one another's breath.

"Thanks..." He said quietly as he slowly leaned in.

"Don't mention it." She muttered in response as the gap closed between them. Their lips brushed together and Gabriella felt her herself leaning a bit more into the kiss as she closed her eyes. She couldn't think then. She was unable to pull away. Ace felt comfortably warm as he slowly wrapped his arms around her, bringing her closer. Just as quickly as it started, the kiss ended. Ace pulled away completely and looked over at the ballroom. He stood rigid, and was staring as if a ghost would pop out at any moment. Gabriella was quickly pulled to the realization that someone was watching, or had been watching.

"What's wrong?" She asked.

"Nothing. I just thought I saw someone." He answered. Gabriella could see the cogs in his head turning as he was pulled deep into his thoughts.

Little did they both know that behind the red curtain that hung just inside the ballroom leading to the balcony stood a very shocked older brother alongside a vicious snake.

Chapter 16: *Conflicts*

Queen Isabel

Mid-Fall

Queen Isabel was currently pacing. She was biting her lip almost as if trying to chew it off completely. She was completely distraught, and disappointed in herself and Kieron. She had had a gut feeling, even in the beginning, that he was not someone to put faith in. She knew now that he was certainly not trustworthy. He had done something that could not be overlooked. She had received word earlier that had disturbed her to the core.

"Your Majesty," she recalled one of her messengers telling her earlier that day, "I have grave news."

"What is it?" She remembered asking.

"It is Kieron, Malady. He… he has infiltrated and taken over Empress Cicely's land. Word from one of our spies is that he charged in and overran her army in one night. We believe she is being held hostage at the moment."

She had been so shocked from the news that she just could not wrap her head around the situation. She had finally stood and began the pacing that she had tirelessly continued for an hour or so now. Isabel had her jaw clenched tight and was fruitlessly thinking of what to do. She realized that she could not outright attack, nor try to save Cicely. Kieron wanted her to, was urging her to attempt so he could retaliate. She had thought of just outright declaring war, of gaining forces and attacking with Arsen, Gabriella and Ace. Maybe then they could defeat him once and for all. No. She refused to believe war could solve such an issue. Isabel came to the risky conclusion of simply requesting Kieron to stop. If it happened to work, all would be well and no one would get hurt. If it happened to backfire, still, no one got hurt. If she could manage to keep him from expanding and conquering she could request help and fix the issue with more thought. Appeasement. It seemed to be the only realistic option. However, the queen still could not believe she had backed up this man. She was ashamed of herself for speaking out against the other *Duces.* She had defended him and told them he meant no harm, that he was only being cautious. She knew now that he was indeed an evil man.

***

Empress Cicely

"Is he gone yet?" Cicely asked, a bit irritated with the man before her.

"Yes, but if he hadn't been you would have blown the plan I had so carefully thought out." The man said, stepping forward into the light. His eyes glistened like fire from the soft glow of the single light bulb hanging from the ceiling.

Cicely simply rolled her eyes before shooting glaring at him, "Great. Untie me then already." She had been tied up for the last three hours. Kieron had come up with a plan to fake an invasion to cause distress in all the kingdoms.

He had told me this was only stage one of the plan. If this was only stage one then how many more stages are there? Just how meticulous is this guy? She thought.

The reason she was tied up and "interrogated" was because Kieron had somehow known a spy was present. He did not know who the spy was for, only that there was one. He leaned in to untie Cicely. As he bent down she could distinctly smell blood and smoke from his clothing. It was a pungent smell that had made her wonder just where he had been before his "invasion". The smell also forced her to remember why she had decided to team up with this monstrous man.

She had received an anonymous letter containing things that caught her attention, as well as information that made her wonder just how he got it. He had offered her more power, more land and most importantly revenge. She craved revenge on her most hated rival, and her most loathed enemy. *Isabel*. Cicely hated Isabel ever since the incident that had occurred in the Lab before the war. Isabel had done the unforgivable. She acts so high and mighty, but she would sacrifice the innocent for her own protection if she needed to. She vaguely remembered the days of the Lab unlike Kieron, who remembered everything that had occurred. Cicely only had that one horrible experience burned into her memory. She vowed revenge ever since that day and now she finally would have it through the means of a vicious war. After she had vowed her alliance, Kieron told her that she was a key asset, but a second choice. To Cicely's surprise, Gabriella had been his first choice. Even though she had declined Kieron did not lose hope. He had said he knew she would join our side in due time. Cicely had decided-cleverly so-not to argue with him on this subject or any subject for that matter.

"Why are we causing unneeded distress? Shouldn't we be laying low?"

"We are laying low. Well, you are. Everyone will believe you to be my hostage. All focus will be on you," he told, pointing a finger at her, "yet, it won't be. You see, all eyes will be on where they think you are, but not where you will actually be."

"Go on..." She said, rubbing her reddened wrists from the restraints as she watched him. Kieron pulled up a seat and sat in it backwards, facing the Empress.

"Everyone now knows I am the bad guy. How devious and manipulative I am. For example; this situation we are in. I have invaded your kingdom and taken you hostage, but only a few days ago I was your arrival partner at Ace's party. All eyes are on us now. We have to take advantage of the opportunities given. You already know what you are to do in stage two, so stage three will have to be quick, but also very violent. Just remember your jobs and I will handle everything behind the curtain." He explained.

"What exactly is going to happen stage three anyway?" Cicely asked curiously.

"Stage three will be conducted immediately after stage two." He told, holding up three fingers then switching to two for indication, "You will cease using your powers two days following the completion of stage two and I will then announce your execution." He gave a devious smirk and shrugged, "but, I doubt I will need to announce anything. They'll surely be able to tell that you're gone if you hide your *aura*. All will be in turmoil. You will then focus on our work. Experimenting and inventing tools we need. Then, Cicely, you will be behind the scenes whilst I make my appearances and continue with our arrangements for the domination of *Anastasis*."

Cicely had known beforehand just how frightening this man was, but ever since joining sides with him she has recognized just how well thought out everything is. He even has backup plans for backup plans. One idea is based off of how each *Dux* acts with one another. He is constantly ten steps ahead as if he know exactly what will happen when he tips the starting domino. However, it will be revealed just how well his plan works when stage two is put into action.

***

Emperor Jaden

Ace had come to my kingdom seeking answers and had refused to leave until he was satisfied. Erika stood behind me as I sat on my couch. I was leaning forward with my elbows on the coffee table and my fingers intertwined, covering my mouth as I listened intently to the boy who sat across from me. He was dressed casually with a hunter green beanie on his head that matched his jeans. His light gray sweater was a little baggy on him and he had brown shoes and a belt. Steam climbed the air between us, originating and merging together above the two fresh cups of tea that Erika had made. I watched as the boy told me about his interest in the tattoos on our body. He had come to find out what they mean. He was curious and willing to learn. That is what I liked about him.

"I'll inform you with what I know and as far as my knowledge about the subject extends. Other than that, you will have to research them yourself." I told him before picking up my cup and sipping the white tea that it held. Ace picked his up as well and sipped. His eyes closed briefly before he took another long, drawn out sip. "Erika, if you wouldn't mind grabbing the book that holds the information about the tattoos?" I requested, turning my head to meet her eyes. She nodded curtly and walked off to obtain the history book.

I saw Ace look at my right arm. My sleeves were rolled up and my tattoo on the inside of my wrist was visible. I was dressed casually in a blue plaid button up dress shirt with the sleeves rolled up. "I vaguely remember Isabel's, Gabriella's, Arsen's, Kaitlyn's and Kieron's." He informed. I gave a quick nod at the information.

"Kieron's?" I inquired.

"Only the top." Ace answered. I was certainly intrigued now. Especially in regards to what Kaitlyn's tattoo was. Erika entered the room once more and set the book down on the coffee table between the two of us.

"Fantastic. Thank you darling." I said, picking up the history book to the desired page. The page corners were creased where I had marked what I believed was most important.

"Darling?" Ace asked, catching me off guard. Erika flushed and looked away as Ace cast a skeptical look to her.

"Yes, I call all of my maids and such darling. It is more of a habit now." I lied. Ace raised an eyebrow, obviously unimpressed with my lie. I cleared my throat and changed the subject quickly, "Here it is; 'West African Adrinka Symbols'." I read. Ace moved around the table and was sitting by me in an instant, looking at the symbols and meanings on the page.

"Mind showing me your tattoo, Ace?" I asked, looking to the young ruler. Ace nodded hastily and stood, lifting his light gray sweater and the tight white shirt underneath. I rolled my eyes as Erika gasped quietly and swallowed awkwardly. Underneath his shirt Ace was well toned. *Very* well-toned. However, what caught my attention was the tattoo. It was fairly large and consisted of five circles. The centralized circle was surrounding his belly button, while two were connecting on each side. I studied it briefly before I looked to the book.

"Well?" He questioned as he pulled down his shirt and sat beside me. "What does it mean?"

"Loyalty." I answered, "Fitting, don't you think?" I said with a smile.

"What about yours?" Ace asked, gesturing to my wrist. I glanced down at my own tattoo. The black ink was a crescent shape atop three flattened ovals.

"Vigilance." I answered after discovering my own mark in the book. Ace nodded, looking over the symbols himself as if searching for a certain mark.

"What about this one?" Ace pointed to a strange squiggly mark.

"It mean's initiative... is that Arsen's?" I queried.

Ace only nodded, gazing over the symbols before grabbing a pen off of the coffee table. "I'm going to label who has what mark and where it is. I don't know if the placement will help, but it's worth a shot." I watched as the Pharaoh labeled six out of nine symbols and circled the ones that he didn't know. "You label what they mean. I am dead set on finding this out. I don't care how long I stay here." I rolled my eyes at the boys determined words and labeled each of the meanings.

"Wait, how do you know what Gabriella's is? Even though it's placed on the left side of her lower abdomen?" I asked curiously.

Ace flushed a moment, "It's not what you think! She wears casual clothes and sometimes they include crop tops so just... shut up it's not what you think! Her tattoo means courage, right?"

I gave him a suspicious raised eyebrow, but returned my attention to the labels. "So as of now we have Gabriella, you, me, Arsen, Isabel and... Kaitlyn?"

Ace nodded, "I saw hers at the party. Same with the top of Kieron's."

“So, you don’t know if his is the mercy or perseverance?” I asked.

“I think it is perseverance... he isn’t one for mercy. But, then that leaves Aurora and Cicely, and I don’t know anything at all about where Cicely’s mark is.” Ace informed.

I sighed and ran a hand through my hair, “From your description of what you saw on Kaitlyn's wrist her tattoo has to be endurance. These tattoos make sense for some of the *Duces*, but for others... I just don't understand.”

“Well, it leaves three tattoos right? I guess we just have to be patient.”

“Indeed.” I confirmed as I took another long sip of my tea. Ace stood to leave, finishing his own cup of tea.

“Before I leave...” Ace began, turning his back toward me, “Do you know anything about Arsen's past? Before the war, like, during the experiments?” I was taken aback by his question and wondered what exactly he had heard about his elder brother.

“No. I would’ve thought Arsen and you knew everything about one another.” I replied. I instantly regretted it because a hurt look flashed across his face for a brief moment. Just what had he heard?

***

A figure loomed in the treetops of somewhere unknown dressed in all black. Their hood was up and their bow and arrow slung over shoulder. The ominous figure sat crouched and waiting for their next victim in one of the many tall trees. The individual then saw its target, a man that had wandered into the woods. It was a noble from a certain kingdom. He had an eagle badge sewn over his heart onto the shirt he wore. Isabel’s kingdom. The assailant slowly raised a fist. Suddenly, they were surrounded by hundreds of what looked to be ninjas. At the same time a green, cloudy smoke poured in and fenced in the lost visitor. The man from Eagle Kingdom began to erupt in terror as he recognized the mist that now had him surrounded. The leader of the assailants watched closely as the haze was absorbed by the man’s skin and took effect almost immediately. The man looked around wildly as he began to sputter incoherent words and screaming. It was as if he were trapped in his worst nightmare. He tore at his hair, his body shaking violently. His eyes searched the woods around him frantically. The hooded leader dropped down in front of the man, causing him to jump back with a startled cry.

"Boo." The leader whispered, looking directly into the man's eyes. The noble then let out a terrible, blood curdling scream before stopping abruptly. He fell backwards, lifeless, onto the forest ground with a sickening *thud.*

Chapter 17: *Siblings*

King Arsen

I looked out of my study window at the deep blue sky. The trees swayed in the breeze, sending yellow, brown, red, and orange leaves fluttering by. It was fall, late October, and a few months have passed. The tension among the *Duces* still ran high and that worries me. But, Ace in particular is worrying me the most. He had been acting differently which has been making me concerned. He has become unusually distant and grumpy. He interrupts me on anything I say and screams at me before storming out. It seems he's starting fights because he can, or is he actually angry with me over something? Maybe he was angry I beat him in practice, but that's not like him at all. I asked him to come over today to talk about strategy and other things about the kingdoms. I heard him come in through the front doors of my castle and being unusually rude to my *Regiis.* I checked the time on the clock Jaden had made, It read six o'clock in the afternoon. I had asked him to come in around noon. He was *very* late. It made me a little angry that he purposely had come in late and his recent mood, so I decided to take matters into my own hands. I stood and walked out of my study into the living room. He came in moments later and sighed irritably before plopping down in the seat across from me.

"Ace why-" I attempted.

"Because you don't own me, Arsen," He interrupted, "I'm a grown man and I have things to do."

"But, you told me you'd come over around noon. You're never late." I told him, trying to keep my cool.

He just shrugged. "Doesn't matter. I'm here now right? What did you want anyway?"

I reigned in my anger and urged on the conversation I wanted to have with him, "I wanted to speak to you about the growing tension in the kingdoms. The weird letters only certain *Duces* are getting, and Kieron's invasion. I wanted to give you advice on those subjects in particular."

Ace looked uninterested, "I don't need your advice. Besides, who cares? Why don't you just worry about yourself and I'll worry about myself. It's easier that way."

I stood up suddenly, feeling rage well up and words gush out of my mouth, "What is wrong with you lately? Don't you remember everything I've-"

"No!" Ace yelled, cutting me off as he stood abruptly, "Why do you have to baby me all the time?"

"Because you still *are* a child, Ace! You still act like one! Mom told me to look after you and that's exactly what I'm going to do!" I bellowed back.

"Well, what if I don't need you anymore?!" Ace roared, the vein in his neck popping out.

The room was silent. I looked at him in shock, unable to respond. He stared at me wide eyed a moment before quickly masking his emotions and storming out of the room. His *aura* was out of the castle in seconds.

Chapter 18: Regrets

Pharaoh Ace

Ever since I had received that letter three months ago, I have been angry. I have tried to keep my cool by focusing on my duty as a *Dux* by continuing ore production, softening and hardening the earth when needed, and construction. However, I cannot seem to get the idea about the letter out of my head. It was signed anonymous and it read:

> Pharaoh Ace,
>
> I have sent this letter in hopes of enlightening you. I have witnessed your talks with your brother, whether you have noticed or not. I have *seen* how he treats you; like a child. He talks down to you as if you need to learn from the small mistakes you've made, as if you cannot learn yourself. Let me tell you why he has been mothering you. He desires power. He believes if he can control you, he can soon use you as a pawn. He intends to use you as a disposable soldier, especially in recent times with such rumors of war spreading about. Now, do not think this letter is a tool to spread a rumor of your brother. This letter was written to you in hopes of showing you the true light your brother stands in. He doesn't love you. He only wants to use you as he had used all of us. I suggest you break ties with him now, because he will only continue these acts and continue to take advantage of your trust. You are your own person, your own man. He does not seek to help. He seeks to hurt. Just remember all of his excuses for having you learn techniques of war and only basic teachings of politics. He doesn't want you understanding anything more than what he can control. Remember this well Pharaoh, Arsen has a dark past that only few know of. A past that involves manipulation and evil deeds. I hope you understand the things I have informed and can now clarify his actions for yourself.
>
> -Anonymous

This letter speaks truth. At first I didn't want to believe any of it, but as the days progressed I began to think about all the small excuses that had passed over my head. How he didn't want me to learn more about politics because he knows how "dangerous" they can be. I had thought nothing of it. I figured that he was protecting me as usual. I now know that the excuse was to make sure I didn't get too involved so he could keep me ignorant to everything happening in the kingdoms. Arsen only taught me war techniques and fighting. His training procedures were probably not only to keep tabs on my strengths, but so I stayed just weak enough so that if he needed, he could kill me. He wants complete control over an ignorant fool, and I am the fool! Well not anymore. I refuse to let him have power over me. And what about his "dark past"? What has he been hiding from me... from everyone?! What had he done that was so bad? His "evil deeds"? I will find out and he will not deceive me any longer. I can't trust my own brother anymore, I can't trust anyone.

I am distraught. The thought of Arsen using me broke my heart. I felt my chest tighten at the thought. It hurt to know now that I was being used, and it still does. I don't want to be around him anymore. However, my wish didn't last too long. I had received a message that he had wanted to meet at noon to talk about war strategies. I had thought long and hard over the issue and changed my mind a multitude of times. Nevertheless, I had decided to go... six hours late. I didn't care then, in fact I was still infuriated with my discovery. I had been rude and heartless toward him, thinking he deserved it. But, I had felt horrible about his treatment when I had arrived home that same day. Little did I know about the consequences that follow from holding grudges.

***

Queen Isabel

I was sitting with King Arsen in my lounge room discussing the growing controversy. He and I agreed on almost everything, especially the strange letter Gabriella had gotten. I glanced outside a moment and stood.

"Shall we step outside and speak? It's a beautiful fall evening." I offered. He stood as well and nodded. We both walked out of the lounge and onto the deck. My patio was brick and led to my enormous personal pool. It was perfect for summers and the built in hot tub could also be used for the beginnings of fall when it was not too cool outside. The pool was surrounded by the ocean and few trees here and there. My castle was on the end of a cape, and the ocean gave a perfect view of the horizon. Nevertheless, it was mid-November and too cold outside to do anything other than talk or eat outdoors. I sat across from Arsen. We both sat in the large, red lounge chairs. He was gazing off into the distance, looking to the sky as if searching for an answer. Arsen and I suddenly went silent and gazed in the direction of Cicely's territory.

"You felt that too, right?" Arsen asked, his eyes as wide as saucers. I only nodded in response. Cicely's *aura* had disappeared. An *aura* disappearing could only mean one thing; Cicely had died.

"It had to have been Kieron." I started, breaking the long silence.

"She can't actually be dead... can she?" Arsen tried even though we both knew that was highly improbable. Isabel felt her chest contract and clenched her jaw.

"We can't let him get away with this."

"I agree, but calm down and let's think about this rationally."

"I know... I know." I shook my head and pushed my emotions aside for the time being. However, I could still feel the tears trying to force their way out. I wanted to rush to Cicely's territory and kill Kieron myself. To slice him into shreds so he could never hurt anyone again.

"I'm expecting a war, Bell..." He said softly, breaking me from my thoughts.

"I am as well," I replied with a sigh, "Kieron is obviously at the heart of these recent events. His letter to Gabriella and his invasion of Cicely."

"Makes me wonder who else received a letter. There's no way he wouldn't have a backup plan for this sort of shaky alliance."

I nodded, watching him a moment, "He is not the type to walk into a war zone without some sort of plan. He knows who else will become his allies and who will become his enemies. He has to."

Arsen ran a hand through his hair and looked back to me. His eyes seemed troubled. He was upset.

"What's wrong?" I questioned.

"Just... It's Ace." He explained, "He's been so distant and *angry* with me. He told me he doesn't need me a week ago and I've been contemplating how to talk to him again."

"Arsen, it's no use brooding. You should go to him and see what's wrong. It's very unlike him to not talk to you about what's bothering him." I reasoned.

"I guess." He pondered a moment, "What if he... what if he got a letter too?" Arsen looked to me then and I saw a slight flash of fear in his eyes. He thinks Kieron has gotten to him.

"There's no way. Ace is careful enough thanks to you." I said shaking my head.

"But, what if-" Arsen was cut off suddenly. There was no noise, no sound, and no movement. However, we both knew someone was here and they were not friendly. Arsen's eyes widened and he took a deep breath. We didn't speak. We couldn't because of a green smoke that seeped its way over my pool and from my castle. It seemed to come from nowhere, inching toward us like a snake. Arsen looked to me and nodded toward the door to the lounge as the murky mist seemed to make a circle around us. He was using his elemental to keep the air clean around us. He glanced around quickly and motioned for me to follow him. We ran quickly into my castle and down to the basement.

"What *was* that?!" I asked, a little shook up.

"*Euphoria.*" Arsen replied as we walked into the armory. Arsen and Jaden had discussed with me the importance of one in our private meeting a few months ago. Even if we believed there would only be peace between us all we all thought it would be best to keep one. Arsen quickly went into the dressing room. He came out a few moments later in his usual aggressive armor that he used to practice fight with Ace. However, the color scheme was drastically different. Instead of gold, silver and blue, it was stark white armor with the jewels colored red. He saw me watching and flicked the small switch on the inside of his ring, releasing his now matching shield. "It changes to match whatever armor I'm wearing so I don't look like a fool in battle." He said with a small, forced grin. He flicked the small lever again, and it quickly shrunk back to ring form.

"How did you get that armor in here? And how did you know that murky mist was *Euphoria?*" I asked, tilting my head

He looked to me with a small grin, "I had Jaden make me a lot of them along with Ace's just in case." He glanced over to the swords and chose the one that looked identical to his own, "I also had him make a few of these. Now, about *Euphoria*. I know of it because I had seen some of my civilians using it in the streets. I've made it illegal and hopefully the problem will stop. But, the mist we just saw didn't seem like it was there to get us addicted to the drug. It seemed to be more... lethal."

"You mean like an assassination?" I asked.

"Probably." He replied as he glanced over his helmet, "I'm going to capture some and bring it to Jaden so he can experiment on it."

"Great. Just perfect." I growled, "How do we get out of this mess?" I asked, walking to the dressing room to put on my own armor.

"We track the drug, find the assassin, and trap him. Easy." He replied.

"Okay, how do we *not* breathe in the drug?" I sighed as I chose my sword. It reacted quickly and the blade lit up with a bluish glow.

"I'll create a continuous barrier of fresh air around us along with all the civilians in this castle so no one is hurt." He responded. "Ready then?" He asked, glancing over his shoulder as he stood in the doorway. I nodded and twirled my blade in anticipation. As he opened the door and walked out I was right on his heels. We hastily made our way to the exit, staying on guard all the while. The green smoke was everywhere, constricting the castle entirely.

"I'll track them. Follow me and we can take them out when we find them."

We were soon out of the castle and walking down the trail toward the town square. The trail we walked on was paved over and lined with trees on either side. The leaves had fallen and scattered the ground, crunching underneath our feet as we walked. Suddenly, I heard a faint *snap*. I turned suddenly and stopped moving, keeping very still. Arsen stopped moving as well, but continued watching his front. I heard a feeble *crunch* of leaves to my right. Someone was following us. I scanned the area a moment, but everything was still.

"What is it?" Arsen whispered.

"I heard something." I muttered quietly.

"Are you sure it isn't just us walking?" He asked. Just then I saw a glimpse of light. Something gleamed as sunlight struck metal. I pulled Arsen to the side and ducked as an arrow whizzed overhead. I felt it graze my armor just about missing my neck. Another arrow flew toward us. Arsen regained himself and was now on his feet. He slashed the arrow in half before it could reach us. We both began dodging and slicing the arrows as they came.

"There!" He shouted, pointing at the distant figure on one of the larger trees with his claymore. The attacker seemed to be a black dot against the blue sky. I was running alongside Arsen before I knew it. We were ducking and weaving patterns to dodge the oncoming projectiles. We were at the base of the tree now, looking up at our assassin. He was dressed in all black, including a cape with a red jewel on the chest. The hood was up and cast a shadow over his masked face. The only thing that shown was a gold colored left eye that gleamed with anger. As the sun set he seemed to begin to vanish. Just as suddenly as the figure began to disappear he was on Arsen, bow sheathed and blade swinging for his neck. He began countering and attacking that even Arsen had trouble keeping up with. I quickly moved forward and brought down my rapier. The enemy saw and dodged just in time, backing off of Arsen a moment.

That small opening gave Arsen enough time to touch the inside of his ring. There was a small spark on his finger before his shield sprung up instantly. The assassin quickly glanced the two of us over, taking in the disadvantage before sheathing his dagger. It was dusk now, and the assassin was becoming more difficult to see. He drifted backward slowly, smoothly, almost as if he were melding into the night before he disappeared completely.

"Who *was* that?" Arsen asked, slipping off his helmet as he caught his breath.

I shrugged, still searching for our attacker. "No idea."

"I couldn't tell whether that was a man or a woman." He said angrily.

"I wonder who sent that assassin, don't you Arsen?" I joked, my voice dripping sarcasm.

Arsen chuckled a moment before suddenly snapping to attention. His eyes suddenly widened in realization and fear. He whispered a name before running off down the trail, "Ace."

***

I was exhausted. I had traveled for three nights in order to make it to Ace's territory on time. The heavy clops of the horses feet against the cold, hard dirt was becoming melodic as I reminisced about how I had left Isabel's territory. I had ran quickly to my carriage and untied a white horse and took off without another word to Isabel. I had camped out at night to give my horse and myself only a few hours of rest before traveling once again. I made this journey in record time. A million thoughts seemed to just now enter my stream of consciousness and raced through my head as I neared my destination. *Who was the assassin? Why was that assassin trying to kill us? Is this going to spark a war? Did Ace receive a letter as well? If so, why would he believe any of it? Who sent him the letter?* I couldn't think straight, all I knew is that if the assassin failed to kill me and Queen Isabel, they would go after the next best thing; Ace. I knew I couldn't let Ace be hurt. He was innocent. And it's my job as his older brother to protect him, no matter what. I just hoped I could get to him in time before anything could happen.

I was soon just passing over the province line from my land, Lion Territory, to Ace's. The fall leaves were falling, and the sun was just about to sink past the horizon. The land was bathed in an orange glow. The trees and even the leaves fluttering in the wind cast shadows onto the ground. I took a deep breath, trying to calm myself as I took in the earthy smell of fall. I pulled up on the horse's reins, causing the creature to stand on its hind legs a moment and neigh loudly. It dropped, and I stared at the distant figure. This person was not the assassin that had attacked earlier. The new enemy that stood before me was a fully armored man, a flamberge in hand that seemed to cast a reddish glow. However, it could've been the sunset casting the shade onto the weapon. He stood in silver and gold body armor, but what was unsettling was his helmet. I could not see his face due to the strange full face helmet he was wearing. It was in the shape of a silver skull with large gold fangs and teeth. I couldn't see the eyes of my opponent from this distance, but there was no need. It was obvious that he was no ally of mine.

"What is your business in my brother's territory?" I called to him. When I received no answer I dropped down from my horse and readied my claymore. "Do you wish to fight then? I'm not allowing you to harm him." The figure said nothing. He only squared his shoulders and leaned forward in a fighting stance.

Seems like skull-face wants to fight then, huh? I thought to myself.

Suddenly, I sprinted toward my opponent, flicking the inside of my ring which caused my shield to spring to life. The skull-helmed opponent dashed toward me and our swords clashed. Just then I saw his eyes. I felt like time slowed as they pierced through me. They were a fiery red and held a hostile fierceness to them that intimidated me. I was brought back to reality when he began to attack. He was fast, but not as fast as Ace. He swung his sword with such grace and deadliness it was hypnotizing. I blocked his oncoming moves easily as they came, parrying and attacking as best as I could. Suddenly, his sword thrust through the small opening between my sword and shield, just barely missing my head. I shifted myself to the side just in time, receiving a cut on my right cheek. I felt as though my cheek was *burning*. I quickly pivoted away and heard a soft crackling, as if there was fire. I looked to his sword and it was ablaze, fire dancing along the blade and even on the hand of my opponent. Just who was this guy? Then it occurred to me. *Kieron*?

"Who are you? Are you Kieron?" I bellowed. He did not answer me, maybe it was Gabriella... but, why? I had no time to think before this person was on me, fighting with such strength and ferocity. As we locked in a sword struggle I made eye contact again. They were now filled with undying blood lust. He pushed back against me and created distance for another harder blow. I spun out of the way of the oncoming downward slice completely, coming to the left side of my opponent. I then whirled and thrust my shield into their side with all my might. The assailant went hurtling in the opposite direction, landing harshly on the ground a few yards away. I could still make out their figure, despite the distance. My enemy slowly came to a stand and thrust his sword into the ground. Before I knew it, the ground was set aflame. A line of fire led directly to my left.

He was suddenly there, slashing horizontally, aiming for my right shoulder. I brought my shield up in my right hand, making a layer of fast moving wind on the outside of it to weaken the blow. There was a loud *clang* as his sword ricochet off and up. The blow my opponent delivered caused a large plume of fire to explode around my shield, burning my right shoulder. I bit my lip in pain and, at the same time, swiftly brought sword up and swung upwards toward his face. I watched as my foe leaned back just enough so my blade connected with the underside of his helmet, knocking it up and completely off. I stared wide-eyed at the face underneath. *Kieron?*

A look of shock washed over his face, but it was quickly overwhelmed by a mask of rage. He lifted his foot and kicked at me. It connected and sent me flying, along with an enormous flash and intense burning sensation on my left side and chest that blackened my armor. I lost grip of my shield, but held onto my claymore. I landed on my front with my shield a few feet away. I coughed violently from the force of the impact and the taste of blood on my lips as I gasped for air. I was dazed from the flash and the sudden pain that enveloped my body.

"You impudent *parasite*." He spat, walking toward me. His voice was not the same voice I had hear in the Meeting Hall or at the party. It seemed to have an edge to it now. His voice sounded penetrating, which was the complete opposite of his modulated honeyed voice that he had used around the other *Duces.*

Kieron twirled his sword forward once, "I'm going to enjoy ridding *Anastasis* of you and Isabel." I was just getting up, trying to regain my stance and attempting to stay conscience from the pain of the multiple burns on my body. Then I realized I had cut him on his chin when I had knocked off his helmet. He glared at me in disgust, bringing his sword up over his head. He brought it down, and I tried to roll to the side. I felt his sword graze my back, along with another burning sensation. I had gotten my shield and grit my teeth in pain as I slowly came to a stand. I was trying to keep my balance, breathing heavily. *I don't get* tired, I thought to myself.

"I refuse to die without a fight." I told. It came out raspier than I had thought it would. I got into a fighting stance and readied my sword and shield.

Kieron glared daggers at me a moment before breaking into a smirk, "So we're fighting to the death then, eh? I can see you're already exhausted... stretching yourself a bit too thin with that wind elemental of yours, don't you think?" He readied his sword with one hand, pointing it at me. "It doesn't matter much anyway. I'll be sure to make your death slow and painful." He snarled. Suddenly, a surge of fire was thrust at me from the tip of his blade. I had brought up my shield just in time as the stream of lava made contact. The molten rock sprayed out, surrounding me as it was propelled and ricocheted off of my cover. I began to slide backward, being pushed by the impulsion of the liquid fire. I used all of my strength to keep up my shield as the onslaught seemed to continue for ages. I felt sweat begin to trickle down my face from the sudden pyromania. I felt like I was being incinerated when just as abruptly the pressure ceased. My arms felt like jelly, but I forced myself into posture by using my sword to stay upright.

"Impressive." Kieron mocked with a devilish grin, "You lasted for about five minutes just then!"

I only glared wrathfully, dreading the next attack and wondering if I'll even make it next time. I glanced toward Ace's distant palace, suddenly furious. I clenched my fists at the idea that Kieron had tried to attack Ace. That he had thought he could get away with assassinating my brother. That he would even step foot in this territory. I gripped my claymore tighter and raced for the man before me. He pointed his sword at me once again and lava flowed toward me, but I moved fast enough. I dodged and blocked each wave faster as I got closer and closer. I swung my sword and connecting with his. The force bat his flamberge to the side and stopped the flow abruptly. I quickly brought down my sword as he tried to move backward and stumbled away. I managed to slash a cut across his chest, slicing through the armor enough to break the skin.

"You *ruined* my perfection! My Faultlessness!" He shrieked. I stared wide eyed as he became livid. He suddenly stopped talking. He looked right through me as he muttered in a chilling tone; "I will show you just how *horrifying* I can be." He was suddenly on me, thrusting, parrying and slashing his sword. He was matching all of my moves perfectly. I was having trouble keeping up. He seemed to be reading my mind. I would slash right, he would slash left to counter. I would parry an oncoming attack, he would change it to deflect and strike. I went to thrust, aiming for his chest, when he turned and slashed upwards. He connected and my helmet was suddenly off of my head and airborne. I felt my breathing become labored as I struggled to keep up. I was receiving countless cuts on my face and body. He was actually slicing *through* my armor with the heat of his sword. I leapt backward to gain distance and take a breather.

It's almost as if- My thought was suddenly broken by the sound of his voice.

"I'm reading your mind. Right?" Kieron grinned devilishly. "And I thought you were the smarter one... shame it took you this long to figure it out."

"Reading my mind? There's no-" I attempted.

"Way I could do that? It's impossible? Why is that, Arsen?" He interrupted, "Why do you think it's impossible for me to do these great feats if *you* were the creator? Is it because you were one of *them?* One of the *scientists* that experimented on all of us before you had gotten taken in as well? I know all about you, Arsen. No one else does, but I know exactly what you did to not only your brother, but to all of us. You're a monster. You are the one who wanted multiple slots in the back of our heads." I stared dumbfounded at how he knew this information. I felt sick to my stomach that the scientists had gone through with it. It had been a sick joke. A dumb idea that no sane human being would ever do. Yet, they had done it anyway?

"I know that you had the multiple chip slots suggested as a joke so you would not take credit." He continued, "You wanted them there so you could make sure one person became all powerful using the other *Duces* chips! I know it! Well guess what Arsen, your wish is coming true. I'm going to be the most powerful and take over

Anastasis. I'm going to be the sole ruler of all the land and no one can stop me. I'm taking *your* chip first, so feel honored." He was insane. Absolutely insane. He planned to take all the *Duces* chips. But, there's no way he can do this alone. He would need an ally. Does he already have one? Just then a name came to me.

"Cicely..." I said aloud, immediately regretting it.

"Well, now I *have* to kill you. You know too much." He said nonchalantly as he walked toward me. I jumped into fighting stance and readied myself. "Unfortunately, my original plans for you have changed drastically."

"Original plans?" I questioned warily. He did not answer me, only began to fight fluently again. I was having trouble fighting, using only my shield to block all offensives now. I needed to clear my mind. I needed to not think at all. That's exactly what I did. There was a puzzled look on his face before I had begun my own offensives. He blocked and attempted to parry, however, I was now landing hits on him. He was beginning to gain cuts all over his body. His blade erupted with fire once again, so I quickly extinguished the fire by encasing his blade and hand with high pressured wind. He could no longer use his fire elemental. With his hands at least. I gave him a small, weak grin as I continued our fight. However, I could barely move my arms now, and my burns were beginning to affect my endurance.

I was fighting slower now. It was getting increasingly difficult to even lift my sword. Just then a fleeting thought ran through my mind. *I might die here.* No. I can't die here. I need to use *that.* I jumped back again, gaining distance once more. I slowly pulled out my *Item*, a black handkerchief with my name sewn into the bottom corner. I smiled down at it momentarily. Ace had given it to me back only a few days after The Great Agreement.

An *Item* is something every *Dux* owns. Something that they not only cherish, but something that holds great power. It is what can be described as a trump card of sorts. When broken by its owner it unleashes a magnificent amount of power unto the possessor. One is basically unstoppable for a short amount of time. An *Item* can only be made once, and it is made by a deep emotion for something. I had Jaden explain to me that at the time of receiving each of our *Items*, we were not as comfortable or fluent, so to speak, with our powers. So, as a result, our *Items* reacted with our chips powers, unleashing a large bit of temporary power to be used when in need. I figured this is a fascinating feat indeed for a group of teenagers. Although the *Item* is easily breakable, if it is broken by someone other than the *Dux* in which created it the *Item* will only reform itself. However there is a drawback. Our *Items* may have extraordinary elemental power that can only be fused with when they are damaged completely, but once they are broken it takes a toll on the chip. Jaden and I suspected that if used our elemental power would suffer. Maybe even our entire chip as well. It was a risk I had to take. I slowly tore it in half.

I immediately began to feel more and more powerful. I let out a scream as I felt wave after wave of power enter my body. My hands were bathed in a gray light as I tore the handkerchief in half. I felt my body shake and tense as I felt my head become lighter. I no longer felt the pain of the burns on my body. I felt as light as a feather, yet as sturdy as titanium. I lifted my sword and shield, then slowly raised my head to my opponent. I never saw how Kieron looked, but I could only guess it was a look of shock and frustration. I was suddenly taking off in his direction, my sword connecting with his instantly. Wind hissed past my body ferociously as my strike connected with Kieron's sword. Suddenly, a burst of flame erupted and mixed with the wind, but it never touched me. The flames were blown in the opposite direction. Kieron managed to dodge to the side and get distance, but it was no use. I was on top of him in seconds, bashing him aside with my shield. I saw a spray of blood come from his mouth and heard a sickening *crack*. That was when I blacked out. I did not feel or hear anything. I could no longer feel my body anymore, yet I was calm.

Am I dead? *I thought to myself. That's when I heard the light swishing of grass. I heard a bird chirping off to my right and a few crickets. I slowly opened my eyes to see I was surrounded by grass. I sat up abruptly and looked around in confusion. How was it summer? It was supposed to be fall, yet it was a warm summer afternoon. I saw the brightness of the sun pouring down and felt the soft breeze on my skin. Skin? I looked down at myself and realized I was in a white t-shirt and shorts. I slowly stood up and looked around, taking in my surroundings. I was in a vast field with bright green grass that danced with the wind. I looked down and noticed I was barefoot.*

"What are you doing, Arsen? Come on, let's go." *My head snapped up at the sound of the familiar voice. It was a woman, but she was standing in front of where the sun was. I recognized her immediately, despite having to squint my eyes. It was too bright to see any of her features except her shoulder length, dirty blonde hair.*

"Mom?" *I muttered in confusion, taking a step forward. Just then a man appeared beside her. He had blonde hair that seemed to glitter in the sunlight.* Dad.

"Son, what are you waiting for?" *He asked me.*

"Where am I? Am I dead?" *I questioned, trying desperately to see their faces.*

"Of course not honey, but you soon will be." *My mother told me in a sweet, caring tone.*

"No... what? I can't die. What about Ace?" *I said my voice shaking.* "What is he going to do without-" *another figure appeared on the other side of my mother. A little girl. I felt my heart sink and suddenly I was nauseas. Tears welled up in my eyes and ran down my cheeks.* Sophie. "Oh God... oh God, Sophie why are you-"

"He will do exactly what you have been doing all this time, Arsen. Living. Finding something or someone that makes him happy." *Sophie told, cutting me off.*

"He'll be executed! He *will* die. I saw him and so did Kieron. At the party he kissed Gabriella... he *loves* her! Don't you understand how much trouble he's in?!" *I cried to them, holding back tears. My chest felt tight and I took another step towards them.*

"He will find a way through it... we want to see you. It's been too long." *She told me with a smile.*

"All will be fine in the end, Arsen. Trust us. Now come, we've been waiting and you can wait with us when it is Ace's time." *My father told, his voice calm.*

"I don't want to leave him... he doesn't have to die! How is this all going to work out? Why am I here? Why did you sign me up for the experiments?" *I asked, faltering.*

My mother said something then, something that I will never forget. "Never let an old flame burn you twice. Make sure Ace knows that." *They began to walk away.*

"Wait!" *I called out, running toward them.* "Stop! I have so many questions! Why did you put us all up for the experiments? He doesn't deserve this! Please..." *I faltered. They seemed to be disappearing as quickly as they had appeared. It looked as if they were walking into the sun. They were walking faster than I could run. I began to feel out of breath, and suddenly the heat was overwhelming. I felt as though I couldn't breathe. I was sweating as I fell into the grass. I was crying out for my family not to leave. Not to abandon me again, when everything snapped back to reality.*

My face was flooded with tears and sweat as I came to the realization of where I was. I still didn't have my shield, and I was in a two handed grip screaming, locked in combat with Kieron. His armor was in shreds, as well as multiple scratches and cuts that had not pierced through the armor littered his face as well. Like myself, his hair was plastered to his head with sweat as our blades sparked and screeched against one another. He had soot on his face and neck as well as scratches. I must have looked pretty similar because I began to feel the burns again. The power was fading, and I felt the lightness I had earlier begin to falter. My breathing was becoming heavier and every inch of me burned with exhaustion. I realized now that the heat from Kieron's sword was getting to me. I knew this was my last stand. I put every ounce of my being into this final standoff.

I have *to win, I have to win, I have to win.* I thought to myself as I continued my onslaught. Kieron seemed to waver momentarily as the battle progressed. Suddenly, I felt myself being pushed back. I was slowly skidding on my toes as he pushed me. I let out another battle cry, my throat being ripped raw as I pushed back harder. Just then I realized my wind power wasn't working. My eyes widened as I saw Kieron's smirk. We had come to the same realization. My elemental is gone now. He began to envelope me in fire, encasing me with roaring flames. I brought my foot up and kicked out at his midsection, pushing him back and away. I rushed forward to try to keep him from using projectiles, narrowly escaping the trap he had tried to set.

He growled in frustration, "Enough!" He bellowed. A column of flames erupted from the ground all around him. I felt the intensity of the heat immediately, and staggered backward. "I have never had this much trouble with someone like *you*." He said as he approached me. Kieron was engulfed in a pier of white and blue flames that danced high above us. I could not see his features, only an eerie shadow of a man inside. He took slow, confident strides towards me as he spoke in a low, gravelly tone, "You're going to die. *Now*." I felt a punch to my chest as I went airborne in the opposite direction. I settled on my back hard, landing in a heap on the cold, hard dirt. I was breathing heavy and looked toward the approaching menace. Kieron seemed even angrier now as he hovered over me. The heat was sweltering even from where I was. I clenched my fist around the hilt of my sword and watched his oncoming attack. His flamberge was over his head and the blade came down quickly. Kieron's finishing blow. I managed to get up and evade the strike just in time. I watched as his blade grazed across my armored chest as I flung myself toward him into the fiery barrier.

I used the last of my strength to drive my sword into his stomach, all the way to the hilt. The heat was unbearable, and I felt the flames licking at my armor before they slowly died down to nothing. Kieron stared wide-eyed, still in position from the attempted strike. Blood burbled from his mouth and down his chin. A small groan of pain escaped his lips as he attempted to speak. I held my breath, swallowing hard as I realized what I had done. I slowly slid my sword out of his body and caught him, setting him down on the ground gently. His eyes seemed to glaze over, his mouth slightly ajar. He let out one final breath before laying completely still. Just then I heard someone running. I readied my sword, turning the opposite direction of Kieron's dead body. I felt joy well up in my chest, despite the multiple burns and cuts.

Ace.

***

Pharaoh Ace

I saw Arsen as I ran. He was in front of a body that lay soundlessly in the charred grass and leaves. I had seen multiple large explosions of light from my window and had come running. It was night now, and the moon cast an eerie glow across the land. Arsen stood in white and red armor. Some parts of the white armor were charred black and there were multiple dirt stains on his legs, stomach, and chest. He ran a hand through his hair and I saw the cut. It was on his right cheek and was surrounded by soot. It was a dark red color that seemed to be burnt on the inside as well as the outside. It wasn't too big and it wasn't bleeding, but it was at least a second degree burn that had seared some of his face. He looked at me with joy, smiling ear to ear.

"What are you doing here?" I asked in utter confusion, remaining a good distance away from him.

"Isabel and I were attacked at her castle, so I thought someone would come to harm you as well. Looks like I made it in time to help." He said, a bit out of breath. *Arsen out of breath? Burn marks? Just who* is *this person behind him?* Ace thought.

"Are you hurt? You could've died you idiot!" I snapped, taking a few steps toward him as leaves fluttered around us.

"I *may* have gotten some pretty bad wounds, but I wouldn't die in a fight." He sounded cocky, "Just who do you think I am?" He had on a cheeky grin that just agitated the wound on his face, but he didn't seem to care.

I began to reply as I walked toward him, a smile forming on my lips.

***

King Arsen

I smiled at Ace as he walked toward me. Was he happy I was here? I took one step forward and saw his eyes widen. Everything seemed to be in slow motion as I watched his mouth open and his hand extend toward me in panic. I did not hear what he said. Everything was muffled as if I was underwater. I saw my little brothers face screw up in fear. *Why is he afraid? I had beaten Kieron.* I watched Ace mouth my name. *Is he that happy to see me? No... he isn't happy.* I then saw a glimpse of light flash below me. I slowly looked down to see a blade reflecting the moonlight. Then I saw the crimson red of blood coating it. Everything became blurry as I felt the warm, metallic taste of blood flow from my mouth down my chin. I brought my hand up and gently brushed my fingers over the blade as if it were an illusion. Just then the blade caught fire and disappeared. I was falling forward abruptly, the ground fast approaching. Suddenly, I was in Ace's arms, looking up into the crying face of my brother.

***

Pharaoh Ace

Ace stood watching helplessly as the blade was thrust through Arsen's stomach from behind. He could only see part of the face of the culprit as Arsen began to slump forward. *Kieron.* He sprinted toward his falling brother after Kieron's blade let loose an inferno in the wound. Ace caught him and felt his chest tighten. He felt tears stream down his face onto his brother's as he held him close.

"Arsen! No, no, no." Ace whimpered, his voice cracking. Arsen only stared blankly up at Ace. "Arsen, don't go... please don't..." He choked out, visibly shaking. Arsen still lay soundlessly in his lap. Kieron moved away from the two quickly. He thrust his sword into the dirt and leaned against it, gripping his stomach and wheezing loudly as he watched the two brothers from afar.

"Please... don't fight him." Arsen told in a quiet, raspy voice. Ace stared down at Arsen in shock.

He doesn't want me to get revenge? But, why? Ace thought. Arsen knew he was thinking something along the lines of revenge, but he knew Ace could not hope to beat him. Kieron was just too powerful. Ace's jaw clenched in anguish as he looked into the eyes of his dying brother.

"What do you want me to do then, Arsen? Let you die in vain?!" Ace asked angrily, his voice shaking. Arsen only smiled up at him. He slowly lifted his hand to Ace's cheek, gazing into his little brother's red and puffy green eyes with his own glossy silver.

"Live." He suddenly coughed violently, spraying blood over himself and into the grass.

"This isn't fair..." Ace told him. He felt childish and selfish for saying it. "What about our practice fights? What about picnics in the grass while you quiz me on stupid stuff?" Arsen only gave him a weak smile. Ace felt his heart in his throat as he spoke, "There's stuff you haven't told me. I know that you've been hiding secrets." Arsen lost his smile instantly. His eyes were wide as he opened his mouth to speak.

"How did you-"

"I got a letter... I should've told you, I know. But, why couldn't you tell me anything? Were you really using me?"

"Ace, I never used-"

"You did... You can't leave you have to make up for it." Ace interrupted, he gripped Arsen tighter.

"Ace... I need to tell you-" He coughed again, this time he seemed to be fighting just to breathe, "Kieron, he's going to-"

"Who cares?! You're *dying*! I need to take you to Isabel or... or *someone*!" Ace's mind was racing. How could he get him out of here? Kieron isn't as strong as him so he could definitely get away, but who could help? He didn't know of any of the other *Duces* that could heal. Shouldn't his chip have already started healing him? The wound was still bleeding and Arsen was obviously... His chip had to be damaged. Jaden knew about the chips so maybe he could fix it. But, he was too far away. It would take too long to get there. What was he going to do? Fighting Kieron now would only waste more time than they had wasted talking. Ace cursed to himself. How could he have let this happen? If only he had been fast enough.

"Ace..." Arsen managed quietly.

"What?!" Ace yelled.

"I love you. Kieron is going to..." With those final, raspy words Arsen let out one final, yet feeble, breathe as his *aura* dissipated.

"No... no, no. Arsen! Kieron is going to what?! He's going to what?! You can't do that! You can't..." Ace faltered, he choked on the last words. He felt like his heart had been ripped out. Why did his chest hurt this bad? It was unbearable. He felt like he couldn't breathe.

Suddenly, Kieron kicked out at Ace. He connected with his chest and sent him flying backward. "Now that you're done," Kieron said in disgust as he flipped Arsen's lifeless body over with his foot, "it's time I got what I came for."

"Don't touch him!" Ace screamed, sitting up. He was still dazed from the sudden blow, but what he saw froze him in his tracks. Kieron had sheathed his own sword and now had a normal dagger in hand. Ace felt a lump in his throat, watching as Kieron pressed the tip to his brother's upper scalp. Ace was up and sprinting before he knew it. He was stopped short by a large flame wall that separated him from his brother. The snake slowly lifted his head and made eye contact with Ace, his fiery eyes flashing a murderous look.

"Don't interrupt." He growled before continuing to make an incision in his brother's head. Ace felt the heat from the wall and felt himself break out into a cold sweat. He was shaking all over, watching helplessly as Kieron resumed his work.

"What are you *doing* to him?!" Ace shrieked. Kieron ignored him and soon stood. He held what looked to be a gray computer chip in his hand. "What is..." Ace faltered.

"This, my boy, is my business now. Nevertheless, if you want to die tonight along with your brother you merely have to come and attack me." Kieron responded casually. The wall of flames subsided and Ace felt his blood boil.

"That is *Arsen's.* Not yours." Ace snarled as the ground began to shake. Kieron looked momentarily surprised before he grinned mischievously.

"All right boy, but I don't have too much time to play tonight. I have other more important things to attend to."

The ground started to rumble more violently, causing Kieron to lose his balance. The vein in Ace's neck popped out as his anger became more and more uncontrollable. A dirt barrier enveloped Arsen's body and it slowly sunk underground. Ace slammed his palm into his chest, gold plating armor spawned from the affected area as he stood straighter. He growled aggressively as his gold armor slowly manifested itself onto his entire body seemingly out of nowhere. A helmet also formed that looked like a medieval knight's helm. Kieron stood in shock and closed his fist around the chip. When he opened his fist the chip was gone, teleported elsewhere for the time being. Ace's hand blades seemed to melt out of his armor and onto his fists. He glared daggers at his opponent and readied himself.

"I'm getting revenge for Arsen." He promised. Ace clenched his fists on his weapons and was suddenly behind Kieron, twisting in the air. He spun and kicked out, landing the fierce blow on the spot of Kieron's back. He was sent hurtling face first into the ground. Kieron landed in a heap in the other direction after skidding a few feet. Ace landed gracefully in a crouched position before sprinting off toward his downed opponent. Kieron lifted his blade and held it sideways to block the double handed attack Ace had thrown at him. Ace's rage just climbed higher and higher as he began to thrust his hand blades at his brother's killer. Each blow, though blocked, sent Kieron further and further into the ground. Kieron grimaced before letting loose an explosion of flames, sending Ace airborne and away. Ace landed on a chunk of dirt hovering sideways, catching himself. He crouched and lunged off of the floating earth straight towards Kieron. Kieron moved slightly sideways, missing the attack entirely almost effortlessly. Ace landed with a skid and violently lunged at Kieron again, who instinctively dodged with ease. Again, Ace spun on his heel and lunged again. Kieron cast a grimace of annoyance in Ace's direction before continuously dodging his attacks.

Kieron then abruptly caught Ace's hand, stopping him mid-air. They made eye contact, and that's when Ace realized Kieron was much too powerful to handle alone. Kieron gave him a cold smile, everything stopping. Leaves held their position in the air and not even the breeze moved.

"Do you understand now, boy?" Kieron asked, looking into Ace's eyes in irritation. "I could've killed you long before this started. I could've used everything I've got to incinerate you, but I won't. You will make everything that much more interesting." Ace stared in horror at the man before him. He no longer had any scratches save for one on his chin. Though it was healed by a small flame that ignited then extinguished itself after fixing the minor scratch. Ace couldn't speak or move. He was helpless to the man gripping him and could no longer hear properly. Ace was sharply thrown in the direction he was heading before Kieron had stopped him. He landed harshly on his face and chest, knocking the wind out of him completely.

"I'll be leaving then, *boy*." Kieron informed before beginning to leave. Ace whipped his head around just in time to see his figure slowly walking away. He was on his feet in an instant and sprinting full speed toward his foe. Suddenly, Kieron vanished in a plume of fire. Ace's outstretched hand was burned by his attempt at grabbing at the wicked king. He yelled Kieron's name in anguish, in frustration. All he could hear was screaming. His throat was being ripped raw and tears landing on his now burnt hands that dug into the cold dirt, but he didn't care. He had witnessed his worst nightmare unfold before him, but what terrified Ace the most was that it had all been petrifyingly *real*.

Chapter 19: *Winter's Becoming*

Queen Gabriella

Winter Beginning

Queen Gabriella was riding in her carriage led by two elegant cream colored horses along a dirt road. She rode past pitiful shacks with multi-colored tin roofs, as well as poorly made walls. There were tons people either sitting in front of their homes or mulling about aimlessly. Some were in dark alleyways, smoking cigars and what seemed to be a new kind of drug. Others were simply on the ground completely still like statues. She could only shrug it off, looking forward to the road ahead as the carriage neared a large wall. It was at least a hundred feet tall, half as thick, and well-guarded. She began to let her mind wander about what had happened recently. Arsen's death, Ace's depression and isolation, and the recent invasion Kieron had pulled before killing Cicely. Not to mention how Isabel had let him off with a slap on the wrist, telling him if he did anything else he would pay. He was obviously going to pull another stunt that would be worse than the last, given that he truly got away with murder twice. It was outrageous how stressful things became and how fast horrible things were occurring right after another. Gabriella had just come from Arsen's funeral, along with the rest of the *Duces* except Kieron. It had been depressing. She had tried to comfort Ace as he stared blankly at the casket. He had said nothing to anyone throughout the funeral. The only words he had spoken to her was at the end before she left.

"Gabs?" Ace had said, catching her attention.

"Yeah?" She had answered, looking at the distraught boy who had dark bags under his red and puffy eyes.

"I'm not a good brother." He had told her. When she disagreed and tried to tell him that it wasn't his fault he only cut her off, "I was so mean to him... I didn't *trust* him.

I didn't even let him have his last words. It's my fault for acting how I did to him. I made him feel horrible his last few weeks alive." He choked out. Gabriella could only stare at him with a loss for words. She could only think to hug him. She did, briefly, and told him that it truly wasn't his fault. Obviously it wasn't much help because he then began to cry.

She was broken from her train of thought when she heard shrieking and yelling. She peered out of the window as they approached the large wooden and metal door that led to the inner city of Kieron's kingdom. Outside were two guards. They were in red and black armor and seemed to be just regular guards. Gabriella looked out of the front window to see they were *beating* people who were trying to get through the gate. There was blood splattered on the dirt ground and on the rags people had on for clothes. The guards were slaughtering all who tried to get past and into the city ahead. Gabriella swallowed hard and looked around, rethinking her decision to come. The carriage was pulled forward abruptly, approaching the castle within and passing the guards out front who continued to thrash pedestrians as the carriage clattered by. The door was slowly let down after the carriage had emerged through, the screams of the civilians outside becoming muffled. Gabriella was taken aback by the drastic difference between outside and inside the wall. First of all, there were actual houses. Large ones. It was homes for the upper-middle class and were fairly decent for living. Everyone was wandering around, happily almost. All eyes were immediately directed toward Gabriella's carriage. Suddenly, everyone stopped what they were doing and dropped to their knees. They rested their right fist over there heart and gazed at the carriage as it rode by, not rising to their feet until completely out of sight.

"Freaky..." Gabriella murmured under her breath, trying not to make eye contact with anyone. But, something caught her eye. The carriage was steadily approaching an enormous castle that resembled an army stronghold. It was surrounded by a massive moat and on the pinnacle was a large flag with a snake in the shape of the Latin symbol for fire. It was red and orange and was reflective, making it look like it was on fire. As she neared the fortress she saw the *Regiis* standing out in front of the large main gates that lead to the entrance. They were large, burly men that wore red and gold lined armor. They carried massive claymore's with the blades point buried in the walkway and their beastly hands lay on top of the pommel. Gabriella could now see the large moat that surrounded the castle as the drawbridge lowered for their entry. The *Regiis* stiffened as the carriage carried on by and then relaxed when it was well past. The bridge slowly lifted back up and the carriage came to a halt. Gabriella's door was opened and two more *Regiis* appeared, both with their helmets off and in less bulkier armor. They offered her a hand to step out of the carriage.

She declined the offer for help and hopped out herself. Gabriella's black heels clicked on the pavement as she hopped out. She tugged on her snug leather jacket and brushed her hands over her white tank top and bole colored jeans as she pushed past the two *Regiis.* She then ran a quick hand through her long hair, the light curls tumbling behind her shoulders. The *Regiis* seemed a bit uncomfortable in her presence as she walked past. She looked out across the massive circular entryway to the main doors of the castle. Standing there was the man she came to see. Kieron. His chest was puffed out and he stood in a Victorian style vest and undershirt. The undershirt was a red satin, the buttons seeming to barley hold. He was either bulky, or those clothes were from when he was in middle school. Gabriella found the latter more probable. His vest was black with designs of flowers woven in with a charcoal color. His dress pants were also black and and his shoes were the ones he had worn to Ace's party. His hair, as usual, hung down in light black curls to his shoulders.

"Gabriella! I have been expecting you. Did Arsen's death bring you to your senses?" He asked as she walked to the door, accompanied by the *Regiis*.

"I came here because I decided it's better to be on the winning side. Plus, you have everything set up so." She answered with a shrug. He took her hand when she was close enough, but she quickly snatched it away, and walked inside. He followed behind and walked ahead to lead her throughout his maze of a castle. The two walked down a large corridor, making a few lefts and rights in complete silence. Gabriella looked around, taking in the architecture as they passed doors and archway entrances into different rooms. Soon they came to a set of double doors on the left. Kieron led the way into what seemed to be a living room. It was very modern looking and slightly steampunk with the sofas, loveseat and armchair. In front was a large fire place, the furniture creating a semicircle around it. The fireplace was crackling peacefully and gave off a comforting warmth that seemed to eliminate any briskness outside. On the far side of the room were glass windows that looked out over the city and the bright blue sky. Sunlight rained in, casting a radiance into the dark room that melded with the warm glow from the fireplace. She saw a few birds pass by overhead then she saw the red curtains. She felt her heart skip a beat in slight fear at the realization. They were in a replicated Meeting Hall. It was exactly like the one that was in the middle of the Atlantic. The same room Kieron had called her to. Suddenly, she felt that the room she was in now was the Meeting Hall. The fiery eyed man sitting across from her, offering her a deal that she refused. She had tried to kill him, failed, and he *promised* to kill her. Kieron sighed and looked to her as the doors shut. The slam broke Gabriella from her reverie and made her spin around to the noise.

"Silly girl..." Kieron purred. She whipped her head back to where the voice was coming from, realizing he was directly in front of her. He was so close she could smell his breath. It smelled of vanilla and hint of smoke. Not, he himself smelled of smoke. The smell of vanilla was intoxicating. She felt herself getting lightheaded. "I told you-promised you-next time I saw you... I'd kill you." He whispered the last three words, sending a chill down her spine. Gabriella swallowed hard, keeping calm as best she could as the intoxication continued. Her chest felt light now, and Kieron began to seem much warmer, nicer.

"What's... wrong with me?" She asked in a low voice, trying to stay standing.

"Just a new invention I'm trying out... I didn't really think there was any use for it until now. You're lucky enough to be my first test subject." He told her. Gabriella quickly jumped back and glared at him. Her vision started to become blurry and she saw doubles.

"Wha-"

"I mean," he said as he reached in his mouth and removed what seemed to be a clear layer of... something, "this. It is placed inside of one's mouth and it emits a drug. Ever heard of *Euphoria*? I heard it smells and tastes of vanilla and is very, *very*, addictive." Gabriella could tell he was grinning even though she couldn't see very well right now. She slowly reached up and touched her head.

"You... drugged me?" She asked. She knew it as a stupid question, but she wasn't thinking quite right at the moment.

"Exactly. Now, I either let you become a drug addict and allow you to die from you own infatuation with *Euphoria*, or I give you the antidote for it." He held up a vile filled with a red liquid. "In exchange you must swear your allegiance to me. No turning back on me or I will have you and your beloved killed before you can realize just what's happened." Gabriella could feel herself losing consciousness. The room was starting to show specks of black in her vision, and she could've sworn Kieron was turning into Arsen. She became certain as his hair and eye color changed.

"Give me it..." She said stumbling forward as she reached for the vile. "Please."

"Swear. I want to hear you swear on what is most precious to you."

"I... I swear on what is most precious to me." She said, dropping to her hands and knees. She became unnaturally calm. Her fingers slowly began sinking into the hardwood like magic. She looked down and saw her hand sinking in as well.

"No, Gabriella. *What* is most precious to you? Tell me."

"Ace." She couldn't see his face, but he became very quiet suddenly. She was arm deep in the floor now and everything was twisting into a black abyss.

Then Kieron was knelt in front of her, lifting her chin, "I hope you will prove your worth. For your own sake. Welcome to the team." He said, setting the vile to her lips and letting her drink the cure. Gabriella was suddenly fine. However, her head was still foggy and she was exhausted, but she was no longer hallucinating. "Now... sleep." He muttered. Those were the last words she heard before blacking out.

***

Pharaoh Ace

Ace sighed quietly. He was stooped next to the grave of his brother, crouched in the light blanket of snow that had fallen. He had a black overcoat on and hunter green scarf wrapped around his neck that covered his mouth. His black jeans were wet from the snow and from how long he had been sitting there. He had not cried once since arriving. He only sat, stared and brooded over everything that had happened. His cheeks and nose were flushed pink from the cold and his hands were bright red as well. He was so numb. He was alone now and he didn't know what was to happen since there was now land open for the taking. Ace knew one thing, he didn't want anyone else to touch the land his brother had owned. He had a feeling deep down that Kieron was going to take it, but he seemed to be stuck on the thought that his brother hadn't wanted him to get revenge.

Why was he so stubborn? I... I could defeat Kieron. It was a lie he had kept telling himself. Ace understood very well that if Arsen could not defeat Kieron, there was no way he himself could. Just then he heard footsteps behind him. The crunch of snow snapping him from his thoughts. Ace stood slowly and looked to the new arrival.

"Afternoon Ace." Isabel said, walking closer.

"What are you doing here?" Ace questioned.

"I came to pay my respects... to an extraordinary *Dux*." Ace only nodded, hugging himself momentarily as he watched the Queen walk to the grave and set down flowers. After a few minutes of silence Isabel stood and looked to him. "I also bring news, bad and good..."

"I don't want any more bad news." He replied in monotone.

"It is your duty to know. You will be the new owner of Lion Kingdom. However, to make sure all the kingdoms are evenly split we will later discuss the correct distribution. Kieron is our main problem currently. So, for the time being the entirety is yours."

"Alright. What's the bad news?" He asked, looking into her eyes. There was a flash of discomfort in her eyes, but it was quickly masked.

"Gabriella has moved into Kieron's territory and has not returned for a few days now. No one knows why she had left, but we did find a letter in her room when investigating. It was from an anonymous writer asking her to join an alliance. We suspect it was a letter from Kieron and I think she has accepted it."

"No... there's no way she would side with that lunatic!" Ace growled, his clenched fists shaking.

"Ace, please. This is reality. She is now considered an enemy. Tread carefully around her."

"She wouldn't try to hurt anyone. You know that." Ace argued, his voice rising.

"We don't know how she will do under his influence. He could be threatening her for all we know. I'm assuming you're siding with Jaden, Aurora and myself?" Ace's mind was whirling now. So many bad things have happened in such a short amount of time. He couldn't possibly believe a war was starting, given how calm it has been unraveling. Every war he had read about was violent from beginning to end.

"Yes." He answered quietly, "Was that all the news?"

"No. Something else had happened last night. Another assassination."

"Kieron killed another *Dux*?!" Ace questioned angrily. How could he so heartlessly kill people? It was astounding to the Pharaoh.

"No... but, it has affected the Dux drastically." She responded. Her eyes became cloudy with emotion as she explained what had happened.

***

Emperor Jaden

My world has ended. I thought.

I had just gotten home to my kingdom after meeting with Isabel, Aurora, and Kaitlyn. The war was going to begin in a matter of days. Everyone had chosen sides except Kaitlyn. She had decided to stay neutral as much as she absolutely could. I sighed with exhaustion and stepped foot in my castle. I immediately noticed there was a trail of rose petals leading from the main entrance down the hall. I was a little confused at the time because the rose petals were red and orange. I had ignored the abnormality and followed along the trail. I noticed just how quiet the entire castle was. It was as if no one was inside. The trail led upstairs to the west wing where Erika's bedroom was. As I walked I began to think just how strange the entire set up was. However, my curiosity got the best of me. I rested my hand on the door handle and paused. Inside the room was completely silent. I slowly swung the door open, the loud creak from the hinges echoed throughout the castle. I sucked in a breath as I took in the sight before me.

Erika's room was an average size with a large window behind where her bed should be. The curtains were drawn open, and let in a pool of moonlight. Snowflakes fell and drifted in the winter night, laying down a blanket of snow for the next day. None of the lights were on and her bed was gone. In the place of it, parallel to the window, was a large, black, sleek rectangular object that I hadn't recognized at first. I had walked closer, all the while holding my breath. I realized then that it was a casket. Inside was Erika. Her arms were crossed over her chest and her eyes closed. As I came closer I felt as though my chest was being squeezed. The red and orange rose petals were surrounding her body and the casket itself. The moonlight made them gleam as if they were live flames. A note lay on top of her. An envelope with a fancy "K" wax stamp. I reached out a shaky hand and took the note. I opened it slowly as I wondered what sick and twisted words the culprit had written for me. There was only nine words, yet I couldn't stop reading them over and over. They told so much in only two sentences. The signature at the bottom was also confusing, given how bland it way. Yet, I knew exactly who it was.

It's your fault.

You broke one of the promises.

Yours Truly,

The King

My hands were shaking uncontrollably, and I felt a lump in my throat. I gazed down at Erika, reaching out to touch her face. I wondered if she would just wake up and say it was all a cruel joke. That nothing bad truly happened. Her cheek was ice cold as my fingertips lightly brushed against it. Suddenly, I was on my knees. I was weeping for her. For myself. What did he do to her before he had killed her? Had she died peacefully? I didn't know, and I don't know if I *wanted* to know. However, what I did know is that Kieron would pay.

He would pay with his life.

Chapter 20: *War Calls*

Queen Isabel

The click of her heels echoed throughout the silent throne room. With each step she took her dress slithered behind her. The light from the windows glistened and danced across the walls. Her eyes, like crystals, gleamed with intensity and kept their hold even after she had stopped in front of the balcony. Her pale, perfect hands grasped the railing as she spoke in a hard and commanding tone;

"We're going to war."

The words echoed in the air. The snowflakes seeming to deliver her message as they drifted down to the crowd. It was lightly snowing, yet all the people in the kingdom stood before Isabel's castle, creating a long line all the way down the pathway. Each of the men, some women, and older children were in knights outfits and armed with sword and shield. All of them needed to stay behind and keep an eye on the borders while the combat trained knights and some *Regiis* were to accompany Isabel to the battlefield. The war had begun a few weeks ago, but it had been a slow start. Kieron had already made his first move and she knew she had to go help Ace immediately. Kieron had begun his march to intercept Arsen's kingdom, which now belonged to Ace. Ace had already been ready for the attack and set up defenses in advance, but Isabel didn't know how long that would take.

"The brave civilians willing to help, I thank you. However, you are needed here in Eagle Kingdom." She informed. "You will be defending this kingdom with your lives, and I value that immensely. We will not let another incident happen where someone wanders into a different kingdom, goes missing, and is then found a month later dead. It is tragic, but we have leads that his death is linked to the drug *Euphoria*. It is highly dangerous and I would rather you all steer clear of it completely. On that note, we have found that the drug is being mass produced in *No Man's Land.* I am personally apologizing for the harm that *No Man's Land* has done instead of the help I had it created for. I will be expressing my apologies at the next meeting, which is soon. However, I will explain further after I return from the battle. I hope you all stay healthy and safe. I will be taking my leave now." The civilians all cheered at the speech, at her words and her good graces. With that, the civilians made a clear path for Isabel and her royal army. She was on her way in a matter of hours after getting suited up and preparing for the journey on horseback.

As she and her army made their way down the trail and through the kingdom the townspeople were celebrating and cheering them on. Isabel continued thinking of a strategy to help Ace.

He most certainly can handle himself for a few days before I arrive. I have let him know in advance my estimated arrival time. He now controls Arsen's royal army as well as his own, so he should be fine for quite a while. One thing is of concern however, and that is how long he can stand fighting Kieron.

"Malady, I know you are thinking of many other things, but we've reached the border to *No Man's Land*. Shall we proceed?" A *Regiis* guard asked me. I was so deep in thought that I hadn't even noticed we had stopped.

"Yes. With great caution. I have heard many rumors, so I want you all to be on your toes. Don't let your guard down for a second." She responded, letting the informed tell the others who had not heard.

Isabel took a deep breath and looked onward as the two large wooden doors were opened, revealing the horrors that waited inside the walls of *No Man's Land*. The dirt trail led down and onwards only a few miles to a small, rundown looking town. It was rumored to be one of the most violent places, even though it had started out as a perfect small society that was funded for by Eagle Kingdom, Isabel's kingdom. Nevertheless, no one wanted to step foot into the town since it had slowly started to become its own drug corporation for *Euphoria*. Isabel raised a fist to signal her soldiers to move forward. Off they went, trudging into the drug ridden ghost town known as *No Man's Land.*

***

Pharaoh Ace

Ace was stood on the top floor of his brother's, Arsen's, castle. He had gone through every cabinet, drawer, and closet he could find. He tore the palace apart and found all kinds of documents, and other strange things he never even knew about his brother. He searched the place bottom to top, and he was now at the highest pinnacle of the castle, the keep. Ace was in heavy winter clothing, standing with a pair of high powered binoculars as snowflakes rained down from the sky. He was looking out towards Cicely and Kieron's territories. He watched as floods of soldiers were forming various different formations. The very front lines held what looked to be black and red armored soldiers while towards the back the body armor changed to red and gold. He held his breath a moment, surveying the scene before him. The lineup of soldiers seemed to be splitting off into two groups. One was heading in the direction of Ace and the other diverging due west gradually. Ace quickly moved the binoculars to see just how many warriors there were when Kieron's castle caught his eye. Ace slowly took the binoculars away from his eyes and knew instantly how much time he had.

Three days until Isabel came as backup, half a day until a good portion of Aurora's troops arrived, and about a day and a half until enemy forces arrived. Ace grit his teeth and was suddenly next to one of the captains of his army.

"Sir!" The captain acknowledged, surprised at the sudden appearance.

"Send a messenger immediately to Raccoon Territory, Aurora's kingdom. Kieron is splitting his army in two to catch her off guard. Speed up preparations for war immediately and let the other captains know." Ace told sternly.

"Affirmative, Pharaoh Ace." He turned on his heel and began to walk away.

"Also," Ace added, causing the captain to stop and turn abruptly, "prepare for anything and keep a third of the army near the water's edge as soon as possible. Isabel needs a welcoming guest." The Pharaohs back was turned, his shoulders rigid and back taunt.

A war is necessary now, and it's all that snakes fault. Ace thought, his lip coming up in a snarl at the thought of the wicked king. Ace was moving before he knew it, heading to the basement to practice his fighting skills as he had been since Arsen's death. He had his boxing gloves on and was already throwing blows at the punching bag. He combined unique combos as he straightened it rhythmically. Ace was thinking up all the different tactics he could use. Every possibility the enemy could make and how to retaliate. He needed to make sure Kieron didn't hurt anyone else. Make sure he *couldn't* hurt anyone else. He was malicious. Evil in every way he thought. Ace had two goals in mind; defeat Kieron and get Arsen's chip back.

***

Queen Gabriella

Gabriella was standing in the middle of what seemed to be an arctic tundra, a desert of endless snow. Even though she did not feel the briskness of winter, she heard the low howling of winter wind. She slowly looked around to take in her surroundings. All around her was the grayness of the sky that seemed to envelope most of her vision. She could barely see a few feet in front of her with the flurries of freezing cold wind and pellets of ice showering down. Endless layers upon layers of snow. She was already calf deep in the snow at this point. Her cheeks suddenly felt flushed from what she thought was the cold of the wilderness. Just then, she caught a glimpse of what appeared to be a bright light.

What was that? *She thought to herself, taking a step forward towards the bright yellow light. She was walking now, trudging her way through the snow slowly as she gradually approached the unusual light. Gabriella's mind was racing. What could that light possibly be? Fire? No, it's too wet out right now. The snows continuous heavy downfall would make it impossible for even her to light a fire without getting exhausted after twenty minutes. Was it a streetlight? No, not in the middle of... wherever this is. She continued to evaluate every occurrence so far, asking herself questions she didn't know the answer to. Each breath she took came out in a white puff, dissipating quickly though soon replaced by another, and another. The crunch of the snow beneath her feet soon became hypnotic as she continued her trek. Soon the yellow dot once before was now bright and only a few hundred feet away. The light was questionably bright, maybe because of the blizzard. However, one thing was for certain; it was fire. Gabriella began to feel warmth even though she should have been freezing. A few more steps and she was now inches away from the crackling flames.*

Gabriella took another step forward before stopping. She stayed put as the howling blizzard winds continued, now accompanied by the crackling of fire. *It looked to be a bonfire, except there were no tents around. The only source of light came the flames casting an eerie orange glow and the haunting moon above. Suddenly, someone was there. Crouched next to the fire in a large winter jacket, jeans and combat boots was a boy. His hood was up and he had his head down with his palms toward the fire. He was trying to keep warm. The winds caused his jacket to flutter violently, making it difficult to see exactly who it was. Gabriella began to say something when the boy looked up. He had jade green eyes and his hair, although seemingly a darker shade from the afterglow of the campfire, was a golden color. She could only mouth his name, feeling her heart flutter in her chest as soon as they made eye contact. She felt a smile creep across her lips, but it quickly faded after she realized he was not smiling. His eyes were cloudy with emotion, and he didn't seem happy to see her at all. She felt her heart begin to pound against her chest.* What's wrong with him? *Gabriella opened her mouth to speak, but no noise erupted. There was only the howling of the wind, and the steady crackling of the fire.*

She blinked once. That blink seemed to hold a million minutes, because when she opened her eyes everything was different. The crackle of the fire was still there, however, when her eyes opened she was no longer standing in the snow. She felt her heart sink when she realized Ace had disappeared as well. Now Gabriella was stood on ice. She heard the whistling of the winter wind that seemed to become more and more aggressive. The roar of the fire was louder, and the flames stood very tall now. They did not waver in the slightest, not even from the furious winter winds that whipped Gabriella's hair and clothes. She stared into the orange flames. She felt hypnotized by the crackle and largeness of it. Gabriella stayed put. She didn't move as she watched the bright kindles rise with the wind and mix with the snowflakes. She clenched her fists and took a step back as suddenly the flames expanded, surrounding her. She took in a deep breath, smelling smoke as the winds began to pick up. Black smoke surrounded her now. She quickly turned in circles, searching desperately for a way out. The smoke seemed to suffocate her, wrapping around her lungs like a snake. She tried desperately to keep herself from choking. Her eyes began to burn and water. Gabriella looked up then. A figure stood just beyond the wall of flames in front of her. The person was just on the other side, silhouetted in black.

"Who..." She tried, but her voice came out a bit raspy and too quiet to be heard past the now roaring flames and screeching winds. Gabriella could only stare in horror as the figure slowly, calmly, walked through *the flames. His eyes reflected that of the flames and he was in a formal suit. His hair was as black as coal. She felt her breath catch in surprise, feeling fear rise up in her as soon as he stepped forward. Gabriella was suddenly aware of the circle of ice she was trapped on, how the fire could be melting it this very second and she would be trapped underneath. She quickly looked to her feet to realize the ice wasn't melting at all. It was actually reflective, almost as though she was standing on a mirror. Through the ice she saw Kieron slowly stepping closer. His smirk, even in the reflection of the mirror-like ice, sent chills down her spine and made the hairs*

on the back of her neck stand on end. Gabriella could only back up, trying to prolong his approach as much as she could in the time she had. It was no use. He was in front of her in a second, lifting her chin with his thumb and forefinger.

"Remember where you stand." He said in a chilling tone. Suddenly, there was a loud crack beneath her feet. She was falling, drowning. Ice water invaded her lungs instantly, burning her throat and causing her to cough.

Then Gabriella woke up.

***

King Kieron

Kieron was stood on an elevated landform in front of his massive fleet with his hands behind his back. The snake was dressed in a general-like uniform with a matching hat as well. He caught a glimpse of a reflected light in the distance.

Ace. He thought. The boy was watching him from the pinnacle of his brother's palace, waiting for his next move. Kieron knew he could only give him a show.

"Split up! One group towards Aurora's territory." He called, gaining confused looks from his troops. However, they obediently split up in half. One section began moving in a steady pace toward Aurora's kingdom. Kieron continued to keep an eye on the spying boy, waiting until he had disappeared to call the army back together. He grinned to himself a moment as he watched his armada keep their course, heading directly for Lion Territory.

Oh, Ace... He thought to himself with a malicious grin, *You poor, poor fool.*

***

Queen Gabriella

Gabriella woke with a start. Her breath hitched as she forced her eyes open. She quickly took in her surroundings, the crackle of a fire directly in her right ear and the calming howl of winter wind outside to her left. She had a red silk blanket on top of her and she felt unusually comfortable, warm and relaxed. But, she felt fatigued, as though she had slept for centuries. Even now she wanted to stay curled up by the fire and continue to listen to the hypnotic whistling of winter wind.

I need to get up. She thought to herself, desperately trying to keep her eyes open. She felt weary, and she wondered why when, unexpectedly, her memories flooded back to her. She remembered Kieron, how close he was. He had drugged her and blackmailed her. She remembered how she had blacked out shortly after that. She realized where she was and suddenly felt very uneasy. It was quiet, too quiet. There was no sound of maids, or anyone for that matter, bustling about the castle. No footfalls, no quiet gossiping chatter that she was used to in her own kingdom, not even the quiet *chinking* of armor from the *Regiis* patrolling. She didn't even feel Kieron's *aura* anymore. It was as though he wasn't even near the palace let alone inside. Gabriella took a slow, deep breath and forced herself up. She ran a hand through her hair. She was sweating and shaking still from the nightmare. She slowly let herself wake up and take in every possible observation. The window was frosted over with verglas while the stark whiteness of the snow glistened a yellowish red color as the lights of the castle reflected against it. It was night, maybe seven o'clock, yet it was almost pitch black outside. Gabriella couldn't see past the warm glow the lights cast on the snow.

The queen steadily took to her feet, hearing the soft creak of hardwood beneath her socks.

Socks? When did I- She thought to herself, taking a glance down at her feet. Her eyes widened in surprise as she realized she *was* in socks. Not only that, she was also in an entirely different outfit. She was dressed in satin pajamas that were an orange-red color like fire. They smelled of him as well. Of Kieron. Though they smelled of smoke, it had a hint of cologne. It made her feel as if he were a bit more human. Gabriella quickly shook the thought from her mind, regaining focus on the task at hand. She crept to the door, opening it slowly so it wouldn't make a sound. She peaked around the corner. When she spotted no one she snuck out and down the hallway.

"Well this is boring." She said to herself aloud, looking around. There was no need to sneak around when no one was there to hide and sneak from. She sighed and walked normally, wandering the halls aimlessly. She was looking into doors here and there hoping she would stumble upon *something* interesting. The hallways seemed to never end. She took a left and a right, and then another right. She felt like she was walking for what seemed like ages. She glanced down at the soft red carpet beneath her feet as she walked. Her eyes trailed up and along the endless red and black floral wallpaper. Gabriella was just about sick of all this color red. She thought she would puke at the next sight of something that doesn't need to be red that is. Kieron choice of color was constantly red, black or orange.

And sometimes yellow if he was feeling a little spunky. She snickered to herself. It was then she came upon the doors that forever changed this *thing* the *Dux* had gotten themselves into. This war that was beginning or had already begun. The two doors she had arrived at looked ordinary enough, except for the fact that it was a dead end... and actually a lot of things were different. The hallway ended at these doors, it was either turn back or go through, and well, it was obvious she was going to go through to the room beyond. The doors were different from all the other oak doors with golden handles. This one had black wooden doors with silver handles. The handles weren't even knobs like the others, they were fully plated, nickel colored handles. Gabriella felt nauseous. She felt as if this door held some great secret that would probably make her a target. Did that stop her? Of course not. She took a few steps forward and reached for the handle of the door, swallowing the knot that formed in her throat. Her hand slowly grasped the handle, the cool metal stinging her skin. She took a deep breath before slowly pulling the door open. The hinges creaked, sending a chilling echo throughout the hallway.

The room was dim, the light from the hallway flooding in and allowing her to see what lay on the other side. The room was also different from all the others. There was no carpet on the floor, only hardwood that creaked as she stepped foot inside. The only thing in the room was multiple bookshelves covering the walls and a desk that was on the far side of the room from where she stood. There were no windows or any lights inside. The only the light came from the hallway and the singular lamp on the desk across the room from her. She cautiously entered the room and inched toward the desk. There was a capsule on it labeled "1/20" on either side. Gabriella swallowed nervously, reaching out a shaky hand to open the laches on the capsule.

As she flicked the two latches upward and the lid sprung open sluggishly. The airlock let out a hiss as its contents were slowly revealed. Inside was a book. On The front was a man that looked very familiar and sent a chilling shock through her. The hairs on Gabriella's neck stood up as she read the name on the cover aloud.

"Adolf Hitler."

***

Queen Isabel

Isabel was walking confidently through *No Man's Land*, with her army trudging behind her. Each soldier was perfectly in step with her. They all kept their shoulders squared and emotions masked. The queen was impressed by this, especially since every few minutes there would be a blood curdling scream or haunting whispers in the dark alleyways. She knew that if she were to keep her cool, the rest of the men could steal from her courage and fester their own. So, that's what the queen did. She helped her armed men and women be strong and fearless throughout the trek. She could hear their footfalls over the bustle of the ghost town. The metal of their armor clanging together and the soft squish of the wet snow soaked earth beneath their feet. Their harsh breathing was also audible in the crisp, cool winter air. She could see her breath, a white fog that dissipated as quickly as it came.

No one dared to speak. There were no hushed whispers anymore. No other sound save for the footsteps and rhythmic clanking of armor. Isabel began to feel on edge. She scanned the area in wait for the sounds of the town to come back, but no other sound came. Isabel then felt a disturbance. An *aura* seeming to come from nowhere. The figure seemed to meld out of the shadows, appearing as if from nothing. Isabel halted immediately. Her soldiers stopped and were already standing in an offensive positions, waiting for their leader to give them any command.

How could this person hide their aura*?...* She thought to herself, watching the figure carefully. Isabel recognized her opponent. It was the assassin from before. The one who had tried to kill Arsen and herself. The assailant stood directly in front of her now, bow and arrow slung over their shoulder. The hooded figure took out a small piece of metal and brought it to their lips. There was no sound Isabel could hear. There was only the small breeze that whistled past the shacked houses and blew the powdered snow across the sludge-like dirt packed road.

They were there in a matter of seconds. Silent as mice and now lined all across the alleyways and atop the roofs. Countless ninja had surrounded them. Their beady eyes locked on every single one of Isabel's soldiers, as well as her. It began to rain. Light sprinkles of water turned into a quiet roar, the pungent smell of dirt now even more overwhelming than before. The ninja were like statues, unmoving, but all seeing as they stared and waited for another command.

"Just who are you? And what do you want?" Isabel called out to the figure. They did not answer, only armed and pointed their bow in one single fluent motion. Isabel could only glare, she raised a hand to gain attention from her army. "Men, women! Do not let your guard down for even a split second. Keep yourselves protected and waste as little energy as possible." In a commanding tone she promised, "I'll handle this."

Just as she ended her sentence the arrow flew towards her, aimed for her neck. Isabel quickly caught and snapped the arrow in half. But, it quickly occurred to Isabel that no one had moved except for herself. None of the assassins seemed to had even blinked. Isabel then realized that they *did*, they just hadn't attacked. All the enemies that were in the alleyways were now atop the shacks. None of them were at ground level except for the leader. The main assailant slowly raised their hand and formed a fist. As if on cue, a mass of green smoke began to slowly drift in from the alleys and surrounded the entirety of Isabel's army. She looked around frantically, recognizing the drug.

"*Euphoria...*" She whispered to herself in shock. The mist slowly crept toward them as if it were a snake ready to strike its prey. Isabel backed up slightly. Just that one action caused her soldiers to lose all confidence. They began to freak out, asking her repetitively what the gas was and if it was deadly. Isabel was having trouble thinking. The gas looming in on them when she suddenly had an idea. It didn't seem like it would work, but she had to try. She clenched her jaw and closed her eyes so tight she saw spots. Concentrating hard, she focused on the gas, the breathing of her soldiers, and the cool air around them. That's when she heard the gasps of shock.

Isabel quickly looked around and couldn't help but smile in amazement. She had done it. The mist was no longer mist. It was a thin piece of green colored ice that was floating delicately above the ground. She swallowed hard, feeling a bit winded. She then quickly called out, "Don't touch it! Whatever you do, don't touch it." No one dared question her. The soldiers instantly regained their positions and confidence. The assailant stood shocked, staring wide eyed at the feat they had just witnessed. Isabel walked forward slowly, the fragile green ice parting for her as she moved toward the figure in front of her.

"You and I have unfinished business." Isabel declared in a cold tone, slowly unsheathing her blade. Her sword was that of an English rapier. The blade reflected the now visible moonlight like water with a light greenish tint. It also seemed to be rippling, as if the blade itself was actually *water*. The hilt was a full silver basket that seemed to gently cup Isabel's hand. The blade in its entirety was terrifying and breathtaking at the same time. The hooded assailant recognized this authority and took a step back as Isabel took a step forward. Bystanders watched, frozen in fear by Isabel's extraordinary deed. No one dared interfere as the two stood face to face. Isabel fluently moved into a fencing stance, blade ready as her opponent seemed to shake themselves free of shock. The foe quickly took out their bow and readied an arrow. The two stared each other down for what seemed like hours, neither moving even the slightest. Suddenly, they both moved at the same time. The adversary let an arrow loose just as Isabel streaked across the dirt road toward her. The Queen seemed to move fluidly. She sliced the arrow in half with ease before continuing, not stopping for even a millisecond. However, the assassin read all of her movements with ease, sending arrow after arrow soaring toward her and keeping distance between them.

Just as Isabel got close the aggressor let loose an arrow at point blank range. There was a sudden flash and Isabel's rapier was against the assailant's throat, ice shattering around them like confetti. All eyes were on them, the arrow dropping point down in the slushed mud. Both parties gaped, astounded by Isabel's triumph against all odds. The monarch stood breathing heavily, the ice wall she had made crumbling. She had miraculously evaded the arrow by using her water elemental to create an ice wall instantaneously to block the attack, then smashing through it to get to her opponent. Although the darkness and the hood still disclosed their identity, Isabel now had a closer look at the assassin. Their eyes flicked toward the arrows then to Isabel's sword.

"Don't you even dare." Isabel snarled breathlessly, "I won't think twice about cutting your head clean off." Everything was silent. No one moved, and no one heard the next few words exchanged between the two. The only sign of movement came from Isabel as she lifted the foe's hood.

***

Emperor Jaden

Jaden stood in front of the large window overlooking his city, his people and his target. His orange eyes like unforgiving flames consuming his unquenchable thirst for bloodlust. His mind raced through the carefully planned out steps to have his revenge. His mouth formed a tight line as he concentrated and stared into the distance. It was then that he felt his heart skip a beat, the feeling of the *aura* that belonged to Erika's killer. He squinted to see the fluorescent orange flag fluttering against the wind like a flame atop the enormous stronghold-like structure. He clenched his jaw, trying to burn the feeling and thought of this *aura* into his mind when he suddenly recognized an unfamiliar one. He couldn't quite place this one. This one seemed almost unnerved. Jaden closed his eyes, reminding himself of what exactly an *aura* was. He had done some research on the topic and even done experiments when meeting with some of the other *Dux* and civilians. An *aura* seemed to be a special trait that only a *Dux* had, a special sixth sense in a way. It was as if you could sense them from even across Anastasis if you focused hard enough. It is a natural indicator for knowing just where any *Dux* was if you had already felt their *aura* beforehand. Jaden slowly lifted his hood over his head and opened his eyes, glaring daggers at Snake Kingdom.

***

Queen Gabriella

Gabriella was in total and utter shock at the book that lay before her. Kieron chose *him*. He chose *this* sovereign to take after? Adolf Hitler. She had learned about him back before the Bunker when she had attended school. He was one of the evilest men she had ever heard of, and one of the most influential leaders in existence. That's when she heard the creaking of wood indicating footsteps behind her. She stiffened and whipped around. *Someone's coming.* Her mind began racing and she quickly slipped out of the doors of the study, spinning around to quietly close them.

"What are you doing in this wing?" Purred a voice behind her. Gabriella's breathing hitched in her throat and she froze. The voice seemed to slither around her throat and keep her from speaking, from moving. She looked down at her hands that were shaking violently on the handle. She was anchored in place.

"Just exploring." She managed calmly. Gabriella knew she had to keep a calm and collected front around him. If he knew she was afraid, if he knew she *feared* him, it would all be over. So she cleared her mind and let instinct take over. She turned around slowly to look at him, quickly, but soundlessly closing the doors without him noticing. Or so she thought. When she turned around he was inches from her face. She glared into his eyes. Their faces so close she could feel the soft brushing of his breath on her face. *Again, it smells like blood and smoke.*

"I see you're not using your new 'invention'." She told, staring him down with every ounce of courage she had.

"I've already gotten what I wanted from you, except your trust."

"I will *never* trust you." She spat. He only smirked and put a hand on his heart mockingly. Gabriella blinked and suddenly she was slammed against the door, Kieron's hand around her throat. Her eyes widened in surprise.

"I *saved* you. You are my property now and will do as I say. Understood?" He hissed. But, then his eyes softened and his grip loosened as he slowly pulled away. "Don't come near this wing... please." She rubbed her neck, breathing heavily as she stared dumbfounded.

"Sure." She replied shortly, walking past him down the hall. *Please? Did he really say* please?

***

Queen Isabel

"Why did you let them go?!" Yelled a soldier.

"They deserved to die!" Called another. Isabel ignored the raging comments as she walked back toward her grouped army. The enemy melded back into the shadows with their army. The Queen's metal boots clanked quietly as the mud beneath her feet sunk with every step. Her mind was swimming in thought as she pondered the effects of her actions. She knew she had to hurry if she was to help Ace or else he would be crushed. Isabel suddenly held up a firm hand and spun to face them, silencing the army immediately.

"Enough. We continue. No complaints." She turned on her heel and walked forward to the beach ahead, not looking back. The legion followed after and the sounds of *No Man's Land* reverberated back to life. The enemy was gone, for now, and the forsaken town back to normal. Eagle Kingdom's army marched on, soon reaching what was a dirt beach. Isabel stopped abruptly, causing questions to arise before she turned to them. "We make camp on the beach for the night. Tomorrow, at dawn, we head out across the sea. It will take us a day to get two-thirds across. We will make camp on the sea and then end our trek at Ace's kingdom, where we will fight the evil that has bared its fangs."

There were no complaints, only a loud "Yes, my Queen" that echoed through the air. The men and women then began to set up camp, all of them helping each other and keeping busy. The queen took a moment to look out across the sea at Lion Territory, watching as all seemed calm. For now.

Chapter 21: *Unexpected Events*

Queen Aurora

I had only really seen him at the meetings we had in the Meeting Hall once every six months. However, I had never actually spoke with him as Kaitlyn had advised so. Kaitlyn and I have been the best of friends since the Bunker and we have stuck together ever since. She has always taken my advice and I have always taken hers. It was a mutual respect between the two of us. Despite her girlish appearance and her personality, Kaitlyn is a very strong leader and extremely trustworthy. I usually do not think of anyone higher than myself, but she is a very close second. Nevertheless, this was my first opportunity speaking with him, with Kieron, even though it was rather forced. The strangest thing was that I was expecting to see a well-managed army behind him, since Ace had sent a messenger telling me so. But, he was completely alone. Ironically, he seemed even more terrifying *without* an army at his command. It was also a bit insulting at first, until he shredded through my defenses like nothing. I had heard the rumors that he had beaten Arsen, I had even attended the funeral, but I didn't think he was *this* strong.

He had then come into my castle, slicing my *Regiis* in two all at the same time with a single strike.

"Queen Aurora! Oh, how great it is to see you." He mused, twirling his flamberge. I could only narrow my eyes at him. "Don't give me that look. I know deep down inside you're excited to see me. Maybe even a little surprised."

"What do you want?" I demanded, not moving an inch in my throne as he slowly climbed the steps. "Why are you here?"

"I think you know exactly what I want, Aurora..." He told, gazing around my palace.

"Don't tell-" I tried, but stopped when he raised a hand to silence me.

"I will offer you a deal." He informed me, "You either make an alliance with me, or you die." I was taken aback, at a loss for words at the threat.

"How *dare* you." I spat, standing abruptly. I felt my blood beginning to boil.

"How dare I?" He repeated mockingly. "What makes you believe that I'm joking? I am taking this territory whether you are dead or alive." I clenched my jaw, holding back meaningless venom as I stared down this parasite in my palace. Then I had an idea, a crazy notion. However, it could just work.

"How about I make a deal with *you.* You and I will fight, not to the death, but until the other is put in a situation of death. If you win, you may have this territory and my army. If I triumph, you leave and never return to this territory and turn yourself in to Isabel and Ace." I stated definitely, although I was feeling anything but confident. I doubted I could win in a fight against Kieron, but perhaps I could injure him enough that he wouldn't be able to carry on with this War. I could even possibly kill him. Kieron furrowed his brow and watched me intently a moment before answering.

"Fine. But, be sure to hold up your end of the deal when you lose." He said confidently with a malicious smirk. I felt a chill run down my spine, but I hid it behind an emotionless mask as I walked down the steps and outside to the courtyard. "Not going to wear your armor? You might need it." He mocked.

"You aren't in armor. I thought it would only be fair." I spat through gritted teeth, positioning myself opposite of him a few hundred feet away. His sword then ignited, a burst a flames seemingly out of nowhere as he expertly twirled it. He stood straight and grinned like a madman. I closed my eyes a moment, gathering my courage as I slipped the handle of my weapon from my boot. It looked like a baton until I unsheathed it with a flick of my wrist. The whip uncoiled itself like a snake. It had steel hooked segments that glistened in the afternoon sun and reflected the glittering snow. "Border off the courtyard," I bellowed to my remaining guards, "and don't get involved."

Kieron hadn't moved. He was looking around at my kingdom as if it were a play thing. I felt my blood begin to boil again and kicked off my heeled boots. I slammed my foot into the concrete, creating a massive tidal wave of water to bombard toward the mad man. There was an explosion of fire as the massive wall of water was split in two, evaporating almost immediately. Kieron stood in the middle, his sword in the air as he glared at me.

"That was rather rude don't you think? I was admiring what is soon to be my land." He pressured, beginning to walk forward towards me. I felt goosebumps on my skin as he neared. Flashbacks of the destruction and havoc he caused already to my kingdom circulated through my brain for a split second. It was then that his voice spoke inside my head, *You're afraid of me, aren't you?* I felt my breath catch as his grin grow wider. Kieron was only a few feet in front of me now. I had seconds to react. I quickly lashed out with my whip and caught him off guard momentarily. He stepped to the side swiftly, evading the attack altogether. He then swung his sword in a horizontal arc towards me. I felt the heat of his blade as I ducked underneath the attack. I shuffled to the side and faked a lash at his face, quickly moving the whip at his feet. His eyes widened as the whip wrapped around his ankle, the spikes piercing his skin. However, he did not cry out in pain. He only looked into my eyes. It was then that everything seemed to go in slow motion. His face contorted to a look of rage and insanity as his eyes seemed to bore into mine. It was almost as if he was looking *through* me. Then there was pain. Agonizing pain in my head that made my entire body convulse in torture. Everything was white for a moment. I couldn't feel anything except fear and a horrible aching throughout my body.

Just as suddenly as it was there the pain subsided. My mind faded back into reality and I realized where I was. Kieron's sword was blazing against my face, neck and chest. I was breathing heavily and a cold sweat had broken out all over my body. He was standing above me with his blade pointing at my heart as I writhed in his unforgiving gaze.

"Surrender now or die." He hissed. I could only nod in agreement, unable to speak. "Good." Kieron stated, "Now, as a new ally of mine, you will give me all of your resources, economy and military power." I could only glare at him as I slowly relaxed, showing I had given up. He withdrew his sword and nodded to me. "Good choice." Suddenly, I kicked out at his legs and tripped him. He lost balance and in that split second I quickly got up and put space between us.

"I am *not* going to give up my kingdom that easily!" I declared, readying my whip. He only glowered at me before smirking. I couldn't believe my eyes. He was *smiling*.

"I was hoping you'd make this a bit more interesting." He chuckled, getting in a fighting stance as well. Kieron then lunged towards me. I swiftly backed up, using my whip to keep him at bay. His sword suddenly lit up with flames again, the heat radiating and rippling the air as he slithered closer with each attack. I twirled in a circle, my whip wrapping around his blade. I smirked to myself and snapped my wrist to the right, attempting to pry his weapon away. He didn't budge. He only smiled mischievously as he jerked his sword towards himself. I let out a cry as I felt myself jolt towards him. I watched my whip begin to glow bright red as the immense heat climbed its way up my whip. I grit my teeth and tried to hold my ground as I slowly slid towards him. The heat began to burn my hand, but I held tight. I fought the pain as I desperately clung to my only weapon. Kieron only continued to drag me closer, slowly winding my whip around his blade. I made ice form around my feet to try to prevent myself from moving. Each time he would flick his free hand toward my feet and melt the ice. I grit my teeth and formed more ice around my whip and attempt to cool it down. I stared in horror as it began melting as quickly as I could form it. I looked up and made eye contact. His fire filled eyes were overflowing with determination. The handle of my weapon was scalding my hand now. I couldn't take it anymore. My grip gave out and Kieron's expression quickly turned to that of disappointment, as if I was a child that had gotten an obvious answer wrong.

I could only think of beating this man. I wasn't thinking tactically as I dove for my whip, preparing my body for a fatal blow. I felt my heart surge as I gripped the still scorching hot handle of my weapon. When I had rolled to my feet I realized Kieron hadn't moved at all. He was mocking me. I growled in anger and twirled, sending my whip in a large arc. Kieron's eyes widened as he realized what I had done. A spray of razor sharp icicles flew towards him. He did a flower twirl with his sword, blocking the projectiles just in time. I felt anger continue to well up as my blood thirst grew. My eyes narrowed as I watched the madman smile as if he was enjoying himself.

"That's right. Fight like I'm going to kill you. Like there is no agreement. As if, when either of us gets the chance, there will be no mercy." Kieron cooed, striding toward me. His voice disgusted me. I continued my attacks, each as unique as the last. However, no matter what I tried he would either throw it back or plow through it. It was all too quick how the battle came to an end. I was pinned to the ground, his blade slowly sinking into my chest. I cried out in agony as I felt fire-*literal fire*-invade my veins. I could only feel intense pain. My head was throbbing and everything began to blur before the intensity drastically cooled down.

"Kill me..." A voice begged. I could hardly believe I'd said it. My voice sounded defeated. *Weak.*

"Oh no. We can't have that so soon." Kieron's voice said coolly, "You still have to pay me my end of the deal. Now open your eyes." I slowly opened my eyes. They burned immediately from the blinding light. When everything came back into focus I realized I was in my throne. Strapped to it. All my citizens and my army were gathered in the throne room. I caught my breath as my eyes widened. "You see, you must tell all these good people that they are mine now." He grinned maliciously, his hands behind his back and his sword now sheathed. My head was still throbbing and my body felt so cold, yet so overheated at the same time. Everything was foggy, and I was having a hard time staying conscience.

"W-when did-" I attempted.

"No. No, Aurora, you must say that they are *mine* now. Try again." He looked at me with hard, emotionless eyes. I took a deep breath and looked to my feet, my heart pounding in embarrassment.

"You all will no longer serve me." I said through clenched teeth, "You will... you will serve Kieron." My voice cracked and I couldn't bear to look at any of them. The room was silent. The only sound heard was Kieron's laughter. His sick, maniacal laughter that reverberated throughout the throne room.

The room was vacated directly after that. Kieron had sent them all out to build up defenses and improve military efforts. I was still stuck in the throne, now fully aware of my situation. He continued to pace around the entire room. With every lap he would destroy something if it didn't suit his taste.

"So, since you're under my command now I've decided. I will tell you a bit about me." He informed as he suddenly sent an expensive vase flying across the other end of the room. Expensive glass shards exploding against the wall and littering the ground beneath it. There was carnage all over my throne room at this point, yet I couldn't do anything to stop him.

"Wonderful." I snapped, struggling against my restraints to no avail. He only chuckled as he ran his fingers over the curtains slowly, a small spark igniting for a second.

"I grew up in a Hispanic household." He told me, "I have a religious background as well. You see, I believe there is a God as well as Satan. But, my beliefs differ from normal, from what my parents wanted of me. I believe that Death himself exists as well." He looked at me then, his eyes cold and unfeeling as he said; "Death, to me, is the messenger to Satan himself. The deliverer of sorts." He suddenly stopped talking. He looked as if he had just seen a ghost.

"What about him?" I asked, genuinely curious now.

“Many believe Death is a man. I also believed this up until recently. But, this is false. You see, Death, or *La Muerta*, is who is to be most feared. *La Muerta* is supposedly a good spirit, but I have met her." He paused again, his voice shook at the mention of *La Muerta.* He quickly changed the subject.

“Death is the one who decides when you die. He decides how long you get to live. Depending on how you live you either go to Heaven or Hell. Thing is, I won't be going to Heaven." *No Kidding*... I thought. "Only because they would all be afraid I'd take over." I rolled my eyes and continued to look for some way out, some kind of escape from this lunatic.

“So now what? It’s inevitable isn’t it?” I asked in monotone, suddenly getting an idea for my escape.

“It was. That’s why I volunteered for the experimentation. It was all so I could become unstoppable. The only person who could come close to beating me is Death himself, but he won’t come for me because it’s not my time.” He seemed on edge, as if he were trying to convince himself not me.

“But that’s his choice isn’t it?” Wrong choice of words. He was suddenly in front of me, gripping my face roughly.

“No!” He snapped. His head tilted back as that maniacal smile began to creep back onto his face. “I am in control of my own fate,” he hissed as he dug his nails into my cheeks, “and now yours...” I felt my heart in my throat and the warm trickle of blood down my face and neck. I began to shake and my mind went blank. I could only focus on the monster above me. The wicked king that held my life in his twisted hands. He leaned close and whispered, “Don't ever try to back out of a deal with me ever again. Or else I'll rip that pretty little chip right out of your head and watch you suffer for three days.”

I don't know how I managed the words. It was a sudden, but brief, burst of courage that bubbled up, “You'll get what’s coming to you.”

***

Ace stood in the middle of the large field in Arsen's territory. He was a good distance away from the looming enemy army that made its slow march toward battle. Ace had estimated a day and a half time for their arrival. He had decided to check up on their progress and make sure they were still on the same schedule. Soldiers were bustling around setting up for the war all around him. Ace sighed as he turned to look toward the Atlantic where Isabel's troops were to be coming in. He felt uneasy about this whole ordeal. Everything in general, actually. That and he was exhausted. So exhausted that he was having trouble focusing on the horizon where Isabel would come. He hadn't slept well last night or the night before. He hadn't slept at all now that he thought about it. He had been trying to perfect his plan and be prepared for every possible outcome. Sleep deprivation was starting to set in and he noticed that his mind would go off in a daydream or he'd almost fall over. He just wanted to lay down and sleep. He wanted Isabel to get here faster. *A day and a half, huh? Can't wait.*

Just then his train of thought crashed. They switched from blistering warfare, sleep and Isabel's arrival to Gabriella in a split second. How was she doing? Was she okay? Is she getting enough sleep? The questions continued to burn in his mind. *Where was she now?*

Just like that she was before him, not quite in arm's length, but close enough that he could see her face. His breath caught in his throat when she appeared and his heart skipped a beat. He couldn't believe his eyes. She was so beautiful. Her fair skin reflected the sunlight like glass. Her grayish blue eyes stared at him emotionlessly. They were glazed over. Her mouth formed a tight line as she continued to gaze at him. The area where the soldiers had been scurrying around and setting up defenses was now vacant. The two of them were completely alone. He couldn't help himself anymore. He opened his mouth to speak and everything went in slow motion. He couldn't think of what to say, what to ask. There was so much he wanted to know and so much he wanted to tell her. It had been at least a week since she had disappeared. It had to have been. He felt like his chest was going to burst now. He couldn't help but feel a tug of a smile on his lips. She looked stunning even as a small tear rolled down her cheek as she turned away from him. Why was she crying? *It all seemed to go so fast. He had tried to take a step forward, but his legs wouldn't move. They felt like they were lead. He managed to make one step forward as she made three. He felt himself begin to panic as he reached out his hand as if he could stop her. As if he could keep her here for just a bit longer. He wanted her to stay. He forced himself to take another step forward.*

"Gabriella!" He cried out, his voice echoing against the barren field and sky.

Suddenly, he was thrust back into reality, realizing he had called out her name aloud. That it had all been a sick daydream. He swallowed hard and panted for air. Had he been holding his breath? It didn't matter. What mattered was that Gabriella had been crying. Even if it had been a daydream, seeing her cry... it only made the tears stream down his face faster.

***

Queen Isabel

Queen Isabel closed her eyes for a split second and there appeared a bridge of ice. She sighed and kept her mind on it so it would not break. *Keep your concentration.*

"Follow me men and women! We're off to war!" Isabel yelled over the crashing waves. Eagle army followed behind their queen, never losing step or even a single splinter of confidence. It was the very early hours of dawn and if they kept their pace Isabel knew they would make it just in time. It was the last day of when they absolutely *had* to arrive to Ace's aide. She had received word early that morning that Kieron's army had picked up pace and were a day away from arriving. So, off the army went. Everything was going as smoothly as she had hoped. The water swished against the ice, lapping at the sides methodically as the armies footsteps clacked against the ice. The bridge itself would crackle from time to time and in the distance seagulls could be heard. It was very calming with the subtle noises here and there, but Isabel was still very on edge. She couldn't let her guard down. She took a deep breath and calmed her nerves then stole a glance to her right at the massive overgrowth on the shore. It was Cicely's territory. A massive overgrown forest that held swamps and quicksand. She had never personally been in Cicely's territory, but she had heard rumors that it was Hell on Earth. All the radiation from the Man vs. Machine nuclear blowout had left many things very... different. The thought of mutated plants and somehow surviving animals left Isabel with shivers. But, there was no one left to fight anymore. Right?

Isabel and her army were halfway across the bridge now. It was the ending of afternoon and they only had about three hours left to walk until setting up camp was mandatory. Her soldiers were breathing heavily behind her, but they continued the pace without stopping.

"We are almost there!" Isabel called out. "Just an hour or so left and we-" a blood curdling scream rung out among the ranks, cutting the queen off mid-sentence. Isabel spun around quickly to see everyone staring at one of her soldiers. It was a younger man, about nineteen, with an arrow poking through his armored chest. Her eyes widened as the younger soldier stood grasping at it as if it were an illusion. The army stood speechless, watching as blood bubbled up from his lips and dribbled down his chin. He coughed once and took in a deep, raspy breath. He looked directly to Isabel and she could see his entire body shaking with fear. He knew he was dying, that he was going to die in the next few moments, and that she could do nothing about it. Isabel swallowed hard and then looked to the left at the vast jungle looming before her. All eyes disregarded the boy, even as he fell back and into the water to the ear splitting screeching erupting from the woods. The only thing that had their attention now was the colossal wave of arrows that sprung from the trees. They were set aflame and headed toward the army. The arrows created what looked to be a cloud of fire.

Suddenly, everything went dark. Isabel was breathing heavily as she held her arms up. She had created a large, thick ice dome overtop of the soldiers. The arrows outside whistled and struck the ice, creating fissures that Isabel had to quickly fix. She concentrated hard and bellowed; "Run! Don't look back, just run!" And so they did. Every soldier ran to the other side of the tunnel. The queen being left behind to keep the roof up and from breaking. Her breathing became labored as the warriors sped past to get out of the danger zone. *No more casualties, Bell. No more.*

All Isabel could think about was the boy's face. The fear that had enveloped him as he stared at her. She couldn't have helped him, she knew that. *But what if...*

Her thoughts were broken off by water dripping onto her face from above. Isabel looked up to see the ice melting. It was see through now and its width had decreased had drastically. The arrows had melted the ice, she hadn't been paying enough attention. There was tons of them everywhere. The arrows now poking through the domes top. There had to millions of them, casting a reddish glow onto the inside. Isabel took a deep breath and looked around to make sure no soldiers were left behind, then she ran. She ran as fast as she could, letting the ice begin to break and crash behind her as she sprinted to the end of the tunnel. She still heard the loud shrieking of arrows behind her. She ran and ran until she saw a bright light become bigger and brighter. She squinted her eyes as large ice chunks and water dropped beside her. They were landing all around her, cracking the bridge beneath her feet as she sprinted. Her lungs burned with exhaustion as she made one final lunge for the exit. Everything was bright as she slid just in time before the entirety of the bridge collapsed behind her.

The queen opened her eyes, panting as she looked behind her at the icebergs she had created. Then she turned her eyes up and in front of her. Her men and women in arms stood surrounding her asking her over and over if she was alright. Her ears were ringing and she couldn't hear them, but she smiled reassuringly and slowly stood up. Her legs felt like jelly as she panted, gasping for air. Slowly she took in everything around her. They were no longer in the Atlantic. They were on the shore of Lion Territory. The light she had seen was not sunlight. It was night now, and the only light came from inland. Isabel stood shocked as she stared at the massive plumes of fire that engulfed the land before her. They were not close enough to feel the heat, but close enough to see the ant-like figures in the distance. She could not believe her eyes at the immense destruction before her. There was no welcome committee as promised by Ace, only Isabel's small brigade that gawked helplessly at the war before them.

***

Pharaoh Ace

It was still morning when Ace had finally come out of his brother's palace. He had stayed cooped up all yesterday after he had witnessed his delusion of Gabriella. He took a deep breath as he strolled to his army that stood in formation. He had on his armor and looked out toward where the enemy would be approaching.

"Is everything set up?" Ace asked in a stern, loud tone.

The lead general stood stiff and nodded, "Yes, sire. Everything is in order and prepared."

"Excellent. We may have to stall men, so be prepared and fight. Fight for Arsen's pride as well as your own for this territory. For *our* land and *our* people. We have to keep the people of *Anastasis* safe from the hands of that evil man. We are going to fight until every last ounce of his ideas are smashed into the ground!" Ace bellowed, his chest feeling as though it was being compressed. His voice was steady and angry, progressively becoming louder as he spoke. His men and women yelled in unison of their agreement, of their will to fight. They were all riled up now. His soldiers were filled with the utmost confidence. They were ready to fight and so was he.

It was then that Ace felt an *aura*. It was close and directly to his left where the enemy army was approaching. He began to wonder just who's *aura* it was. Who would be nervous, this close? He slowly turned to his left and saw Kieron's army, its massiveness was almost incomprehensible. It seemed to stretch the width of the entire territory. He felt his heart flutter and his eyes widen. He wasn't listening to instinct anymore. He had to fight with his brain against Kieron. The entire army before him stiffened as they watched the enemy approach. They were still far off, but their enormous size made them seem more intimidating.

"Everything is ready... correct?" Ace asked in monotone, walking past and in front of his soldiers to face the enemy. If the General had answered Ace didn't hear. He was busy staring down the enemy, his eyes locked on the person in the dead center of the enemy combatants. "Into position, now." Ace bellowed as his hand blades were thrust out and readied. His militia quickly got into their formations behind him, ready to battle without question.

"Everyone is ready, sire!" The General called out.

"Kieron is mine. Once I engage battle be sure to get a good distance away. I am not responsible for any damage inflicted after I make contact." Ace growled as he prepared himself to take off. He took one last glance toward the Atlantic. He managed to get a glimpse Isabel's army on the other side as they began to make their way over steadily. Ace took a deep breath and let his helmet form around his head.

He took off suddenly. In the blink of an eye he was on the first soldier of the enemy brigade. He was in slow motion for a millisecond as the soldiers face contorted in fear and surprise, while Ace's became a mask of rage. The Pharaoh slammed his plated knee into the soldier's stomach, sending him flying backward into his friendlies and leaving behind a spray of blood. Adrenaline was pumping through his body. Ace continued his onslaught of the enemy soldiers. He ripped them to shreds as he plowed his way through at top speed toward his main target, leaving behind a trail of carnage filled with dead bodies and glistening crimson. He was out for blood, and sympathy was not going to get in his way. But, he still couldn't help feeling as though something was off. He couldn't quite place it, but something was not right about this. Ace didn't have much time to think about this before he narrowly missed a large ball of fire. He came to a skidding stop to see the assailant. However, it was not Kieron. Ace felt his heart plummet to his stomach and his chest tighten. *No. No it can't be*

There was no way. He knew something had been off about this about this arrangement. How Kieron had tried to *hide* himself. It didn't make sense. Ace's mind was swimming and he could only gape at the figure before him. She was as beautiful as she had been when he had last seen her. Gabriella's cold, grayish blue eyes stared back at him. She stood rigid in her black chained combat boots and her black plated armor. She looked stunning even with her two deadly brass knuckles, each with a double sided blade on the ends. He couldn't help but stare at her even as she shook momentarily, a shiver of regret and fear. It was only a glimpse, a split second of emotion that seeped through the cracks of her mask. Her walls were back up in an instant and he could not tell what she was thinking.

"Gabriella..." His voice cracked, "Gabriella, you're okay? What are you doing here you're not really working for... him right?" He asked his cheeks gaining color. She didn't answer him. She only seemed to look through him. Then she sprinted towards him. She was fast. Terrifyingly fast as she lunged at him with her blades. Ace managed to dodge just in time and pivot away. He felt as though his heart was being torn to pieces. She had aimed for his neck. She had aimed for *him*. Ace's breathing became labored as his heart lurched up into his throat. He wanted to scream at her. To ask her why she was trying to hurt him. Ask her what Kieron had done to her to make her act this way. He could only stare at her as she slowly stood and turned to look at him. She was emotionless as she glared back at him. She started to walk towards him, her body tense. Ace could not move, would not move. He stood nailed to the ground and watched her approach, her fists gripping the brass knuckles so tightly her hand turned white. Her foot falls became louder as she got closer and closer. It was not snowing, but there was a thin layer of snow on the ground that crunched beneath her boots. He could see her breath. They were short and quick puffs.

She wouldn't hurt me. I know she wouldn't.

Ace's mind felt foggy as she pulled her arm back and let loose directly toward his face. He did not move. His head remained still as he stared in a dreamlike state in her eyes. Her fist stopped inches before connecting with his face. He felt the immense heat move around his head, blowing hot air in and past his face. Gabriella's eyes looked strained as if she were fighting herself, her mind. Her jaw was tight as she let out a deep, aggravated breath and pulled her hand away.

"Gabri-" He tried, a small smile tugging at his lips.

"Don't." Her voice was colder than the air surrounding them. He felt his heart waver and his smile fade. Wasn't she happy to see him? "Fight me Ace. That won't happen again. I will hurt you if you don't fight back." She looked at him then. Her eyes pleading with him. Ace's eyes widened and he felt his throat tighten. *Fight her?*

She turned and took a few steps back, then turned to face him again. She took a deep breath and took up a boxing stance. Ace couldn't believe what he heard. What he *saw*. Gabriella didn't beg. It wasn't her style. What did Kieron do to her? What did he threaten her with? He stared blankly as she rushed for him. She aimed and hurled her bladed fist at him. Something was wrong. Ace quickly cocked his head out of the way, her fist zooming past his head. He felt a burning cut on his neck and clenched his jaw. *She's really going to kill me if I don't fight.* She threw blazing punch after punch, each more vicious than the last. Her eyes became more and more smoldering as he dodged them. Gabriella swung a roundhouse kick at his face, narrowly missing him with her bladed boot. Her chest heaved as she cast blow after blow at him. Ace then stopped moving. He stood still and let her punch him in the stomach. He felt his lungs flatten, unable to catch his breath as he was propelled backwards. He felt a wetness on his lips and his stomach ache where she had punched him. He landed harshly on the ground a few feet away, the back of his head slamming into the ground. Ace's vision became blurry as he slowly lifted his head to see Gabriella's look of shock contort to rage. Sluggishly he looked at his stomach.

Ace's armor was pitch black where she had punched him, and three holes were punched into the plated steel. It may have been his imagination, but he thought he saw red seeping out of those holes. He steeled himself and got up, wheezing. He knew he couldn't be serious, but he could put on a show if that's what she wanted. Ace closed his eyes a moment then opened them to see Gabriella's fist was aimed directly for his face. He ducked just in time and smashed the palm of his hand into her stomach, hard enough to push her back. Her eyes widened in shock as she held back a cough. She flew backwards, but managed to land on her feet. Ace instinctively fell into a fighting position and sprinted forward. He was on her in an instant, a look of surprise washing over her as she rolled out of the way of his hand blade. He felt his hand sink into the hard, frozen dirt. He pulled it free, but not fast enough. Gabriella slammed her knee into his head and sent him hurtling in the opposite direction. He felt his head spin and his helmet fly off.

Ace quickly stood up and crossed his arms, blocking her knee just in time. He created sturdy footholds and covered his arms in rock as she let loose flames around her knee. The stone around his arms kept him from getting burned, but she was thrusting herself forward with flames. Ace growled and pushed back harder. His feet started to slide backward. His eyes locked with hers as he tried to stay on his feet, desperately trying to keep her at bay. Ace suddenly felt her hands on his head as she vaulted over him. She slammed her feet into his back and launched herself off of him, sending him flying forward. Ace caught himself just in time and spun to deflect her blade with his own. He managed to dodge just in time as her other hand swung inches from his face. He grabbed ahold of her wrist and stopped her.

"Why can't you talk to me?" He asked her, his heart still racing. "I'm not going to hurt you. You know that."

She only ignored him and slammed her head into his, his head reeling back. He let go and his hand flew to his now bleeding forehead. He cursed under his breath and looked to her. She was still emotionless as she stared back at him, her own forehead bleeding. Ace felt anger well up in his chest as he thought about why she was like this. Frustration growing and festering with the thought of Kieron coming close to her. He was broken from his thoughts when there was a dull *thud* on the ground. He saw she had dropped her knuckles and had pulled out her twin daggers. Their wicked blade warped in such a way that he knew would cause unbearable pain if he was struck with it. He had to get serious now. Gabriella wouldn't do this. It wasn't her. So he would pretend it wasn't her.

Ace came at her first, thrusting forward with his hand blade. She swung forwards at the same time then twisted her blade in his hand blades. She had caught his weapon in one hand and sliced at his neck with the other. Ace grit his teeth and moved his head to the side, but not fast enough. Gabriella managed to cut him and he felt the wound burn as he stared at her in shock. Her face was still a mask to him. There were so many emotions swirling in her eyes that he couldn't tell what she was feelings. Suddenly, two large hands came up from the earth, grasping ahold of Gabriella's wrists. The hands were made of stone and dirt, something that Gabriella would have to completely incinerate to escape. Ace made them pull her backwards and away. The look of pure shock and fear on Gabriella's face sent a wave of pain through his chest. He steeled himself and kept her in place as his breaths came out rapidly.

"Gabriella... why can't you just tell me what's going on?" He asked through labored breaths. She didn't answer him. She wasn't even looking at him now. She only stared at the ground, her jaw clenched as she caught her breath. Ace wiped the sweat from his brow and took his first look around them. Everything was chaos. Dead bodies littered the battlefield. The once snow covered land was now scorched and grotesquely dug up. There were still soldiers fighting, neither side letting up for a moment as the war waged. No soldiers came near the two *Dux* out of fear. He did not try to talk to her anymore, he only stared at her.

It was then that she looked up and made eye contact with him. There was nothing there. No anger, sadness or even fear. Nothing. Then he was blinded by a bright light. Ace squinted against it and brought his arm up to shield his eyes. He felt a blast of hot air against his entire body and struggled to breath. Ace felt his armor beginning to *melt*, the material feeling unbearably hot now, and his skin burning. He quickly brought up a large block of stone to protect himself, but it began to deteriorate as the light continued to blaze. Just as suddenly as it came, the light died down. Ace looked to see that he and Gabriella were standing in a massive crater. Any bodies in a fifty-mile radius was either scorched or nowhere to be found. Ace stared in horror as Gabriella slowly looked up at him. Her body was ablaze with white light. No, it wasn't light. It was *fire*.

Gabriella slowly held up a hand, a white inferno erupting and heading straight for him now. Ace lifted his arms to shield himself, tensing up for the fatal blow. *This was it, kill by the one I-* His thoughts were cut off by a harsh hissing sound and the sprinkle of scalding hot water against his cheek. Ace opened his eyes just enough to see a surging column of water counteracting Gabriella's bright light. He quickly turned to see Isabel, her hand outstretched and a massive fleet pouring into the battlefield from behind her. Ace felt a surge of hope and looked back to Gabriella. Isabel's attack was beating hers, the column of water getting closer and closer to her as she began to falter. The enormous flow of water hit Gabriella directly. Ace managed to glimpse her body being flung backwards before it was devoured from sight. He cried out her name. His heart surging out of his chest. He was sprinting in the direction the water had flowed, searching desperately for her body. His mind racing, thinking thoughts that made him feel like he was going to lose his mind. *Not her too. Oh God, please not her too.*

Isabel's voice rung out to him just as he found Gabriella. Her body was in a heap, soaked and unmoving in a pool of mud. "Ace, no! Don't get near her!" He ignored her and made his way over to Gabriella slowly. He did not want to see her like this yet he couldn't look away. Ace then felt another *aura*, it was Aurora's. *What is she doing here? She should've arrived way earlier than this.* He looked up quickly to see her in an elegant dress, but the hem was torn and she was barefoot. Her eyes were wide and wild, her hair looked as if someone had dragged her by it. She was visibly shaking as she stared directly at him. Ace was frozen in place, gaping at her. Isabel must have been too because she was silent now. Although the sounds of war still sounded out around them, it was muffled to him.

"You two... why are you here? You need to leave you can't be here anymore he-" Aurora tried.

"We're here because Kieron started a war with us! Why are you not helping us Aurora? What happened to you?" Isabel cut in, her jaw clenched.

Aurora didn't get a chance to fully answer. She had opened her mouth to reply, managing *"La Muerta"*, when a loud *bang* rang out. The sound echoed in the vast battlefield. Ace could only stare in horror as Aurora's body lurched forward, blood spraying from her chest and mouth. He managed to glimpse the large, gaping hole where her heart should be as she fell forward and revealed the person behind her.

Chapter 22: *La Muerta*

King Kieron

Kieron's army marched in perfect unison behind him. It was not a large army, in fact it was rather small. Only one hundred men, all *Regiis,* followed him. He didn't need them really, it just made a more terrifying sight so that the townspeople wouldn't fight back. He smirked to himself as he was proven right. The civilians of Eagle Territory opened the gates and laid down their weapons. He suddenly stopped. He raised a fist to halt his fleet.

"Take them back to my kingdom and check for imperfects." He bellowed. Immediately, the small army marched around him and into Isabel's kingdom to gather up all the civilians inside. Kieron strolled inside and walked to the town square. He surveyed the area slowly, taking in where he would put buildings and which structures he would take down. Soon the kingdom was completely barren. Fifty of his men had been instructed to escort them back to his own kingdom while the other half stayed put with him.

The town square was very well laid out. There was a large fountain in the center surrounded by several market places. The fountain was that of an Eagle, but what made it so unique was that there was no actual structure. It was *water.* Isabel had the jets of water spray out in certain locations to depict that of a large eagle, its wings spread and beak open. A garden surrounded the eagle as well as a brick walkway around it. It was adequate. However, he would change everything in this immense town square, as well as the entirety of Eagle kingdom's layout.

"Come, men!" He called out and began to walk on the paved pathway to Isabel's castle. He only got halfway across the town square before he sensed someone. Or *something.* It had no *aura,* which made Kieron narrow his eyes and stared into the distance. Just then he heard his men cry out in pain behind him. He didn't have to turn around to see that they had been impaled. He heard the sounds of them choking on their own blood, suffocating as they bled out. Their chests were gushing blood, splattering and staining the stone below them. Kieron only grimaced. He was disgusted with how weak they were. They were killed instantly by giant spikes of stone and feared death even though it is inevitable. He turned to tell them how pathetic they were when a tall hooded figure seemed to meld out of the shadows. It appeared to be male and had no *aura*. It did not speak and It's hood cast a shadow over It's face that made Kieron's heart lurch. He swallowed hard and shook the idea from his head. *It couldn't be* him. *There was no way. It wasn't his time yet.*

The lanky figure held out a pale, boney hand and a large scythe took form. Kieron's eyes widened as he stared at the moonlit reflected blade. *It was him. Death.* He didn't realize he had been holding his breath, nor had he realized he was shaking. What was this awful feeling? Why did his heart feel like it was going to burst out of his chest? Why did his stomach turn every time this... *thing* moved? How come he felt goose bumps all over his skin? No. He did not feel *fear*. He only provoked it. No one else could make him actually afraid. No *human*, that was. *Except for... No. That person was not human*.

Kieron shook his head free of the thoughts and drew his flamberge. He didn't understand what he was feeling, but he knew he wasn't going to let this *thing* stand in his way. The lanky figures bright, flaming orange eyes peaked through the hood. There was still no *aura* and this unnerved Kieron the most. If there was no *aura* then It's definitely not a *Dux*... so then what was It? He took a deep breath and rushed the enemy. Kieron sprinted and, when close enough, leaped to the side. The enemy hadn't moved an inch. Only It's eyes followed Kieron's every move. He clenched his teeth and swung upwards. Kieron saw a blur of motion and there was a loud *clang* of metal on metal. Sparks flew as his flamberge ricocheted off of Death's scythe. His eyes widened and he leaped backward, away from the hooded creature. It was fast, just as fast as himself. Their speed matched up perfectly so he could just barely keep up. *But then why does It seem so much faster than me? Why am I hesitating to attack?*

Death slowly began to glide toward him and Kieron felt his heart begin to pick up speed. Suddenly, the hooded enemy rushed toward him at an inhuman speed. It was on him before he could react, swinging It's scythe, just barely missing Kieron's head as he ducked. It continued It's assaults, swinging at him ruthlessly, yet with monstrous precision. It was enraged with him. It didn't make a sound. Not even a grunt as it swung the massive weapon around. Kieron was just barely dodging them. He saw the blade aiming to slice him in two and tried to move backward. Kieron wasn't fast enough as the blade sliced down the middle of his chest. He was only just barely dodging the attacks. He continued to take damage as he took leap after leap to try to dodge. Kieron began to feel something bubble up in his chest. Adrenaline was pumping through his veins as he became angrier and angrier with himself. He was never afraid and he was not afraid now. Suddenly, the mad king began to fight back. He was sloppy, he knew it, but he couldn't help swinging his sword haphazardly. He was only met with block after block from the hooded figure, never able to get a hit in. But, his rage kept building. He ignited his sword and began hauling plumes of flame towards his enemy. The opponent simply blocked them with large slabs of stone and dirt as It continued to block and counter attack Kieron's every move. He felt his confidence waver and bit down on his lip hard. He felt blood seep into his mouth and down chin. He yelled in rage. In despair. In frustration. There was no way he was going to lose any battle, not even this one. He sped up his attacks. Each one was more aggressive than the last. Yet, each one was stopped or evaded with almost no effort. In his blind rage Kieron hadn't seen the figure attack.

The creature had sidestepped his attack and spun the scythe around. The butt of It's weapon connected with Kieron's flamberge, sending it flying. Kieron stared in horror as he watched it clatter on the brick walkway and seep into the ground. He swallowed hard and slowly looked to the *thing* in front of him. He stared up into the emotionless eyes of his opponent. *I'm going to die. This is it.* It's eyes were pools of fire that consumed his mind for a moment as It raised It's scythe for the ending blow. Kieron did not move. He *couldn't* move. He suddenly felt his eyes widen and his heart sounded very far off in the distance. The beating of his heart became rapid at the notice of something else's presence. He felt his lungs contract and suddenly he couldn't breathe. His chest felt like it was being squeezed tighter than before. His legs felt like jelly and he began to shake. *What is this feeling?* He stared up at the creature and whispered a name. The name of who truly made him feel this way. The name of the *thing* that was also here. That had been here the entire time. The creature that made the hairs on the back of his neck stand up. The monster that made him feel that *repulsive* emotion. The demon that he considered was the only thing he truly did *fear*.

"La Muerta..." Kieron whispered. His voice cracked as he said the name. The "Death" that stood before him now stopped mid slice. It's blade just pricking Kieron's shoulder. Kieron hadn't noticed that it had cut him. He was staring past this hooded figure at the real Death. The cloaked attacker was frozen. Ice rapidly crept up from nowhere and created thick pillars of ice that gripped the cloaked monster's hands, chest and feet. It ripped the weapon away and the cloaked attacker out as if It was pinned to a cross. These pillars locked into the ground and he knew there was no breaking them. This was no ordinary ice. It glistened unusually and no matter how hard this creature tried. It couldn't even put a scratch on the ice. Not only that, it was penetrating the hooded creatures skin, turning it a sickly black. *Dry ice.* Just then, two large, grotesquely sharpened stalagmites shot out from the ground on either side of the impostor. They stopped just before hitting It's head. Then he heard a laugh from behind the figure.

It was a bone chilling giggle that rung out in the courtyard. The impostor stopped struggling and tensed even more when it sounded out again. This time was louder and more unruly. It was a loud female laugh that rung out, a maniacal and insane laugh that made Kieron quiver in fear. The hood on the attacker was pulled back and Jaden's face was revealed. His face was pale and a look of pure terror. Kieron stared in awe at him. This was the parasite that had beaten him? This thing had caused his imperfections? Kieron began to feel anger bubble up, but suddenly stopped when the pointed ice moved closer to Jaden's temples. They slowly began sinking in before stopping abruptly. Jaden cried out in pain as he tried desperately not to shake.

"La Muerta." Kieron whispered once more. It was then that she moved around Jaden and into view. She had gold plated armor that looked almost futuristic. The water made it shimmer along with the white mesh glove on her right hand. The fingertips had spiked silver nails that could rip your throat out with a gentle touch. She trailed her fingertips along the ice slowly and smiled a smile only a mad woman could have. She then looked to Kieron, her eyes staring through him like he was a sheet of glass. She took one step closer and he felt nauseous.

"How many times have I told you not to call me that, Kieron?" She purred as she cocked her head to the side. He was shaking uncontrollably now. He felt like he was suffocating and everything sounded as if he was underwater. "You know my name, *boy.*" Her voice was like silk, slowly wrapping itself around his neck and tightening. "So say it." She said, her voice suddenly sharp.

Kieron's voice cracked as he said it. The name of the true *La Muerta*; "Kaitlyn." She did not reply. She only smiled at him as if he were a toddler. She then walked over, plucked the scythe from his shoulder with incredible ease, and spun it a few times smoothly. Kieron had not noticed that it had been stuck in his shoulder, nor that he had fallen to his knees. He bit the inside of his cheek and brought his hand to the wound that was bleeding profusely. It was excruciating. He felt as though his entire arm was being torn off slowly. How had he not felt this before?

"What a nice weapon." She said thoughtfully as she gracefully tried out the scythe. "It has a second blade doesn't it?" Jaden looked at her in surprise. He took in a quick, deep breath and stared at Kaitlyn, his jaw hanging wide open. She flicked her wrist, swinging the butt of the scythe down. A second wicked looking blade to snap out and lock in place.

"How did you... how could you know?" Jaden managed, his eyes as wide as saucers.

Kaitlyn only giggled sweetly, "Jaden, is there anything I *don't* know?"

"I kept-" He tried.

"*Tried* to keep it a secret. I know. I know about everything. Even your little fling with Erika." She turned to look at him. As she made eye contact Kieron could see Jaden's eyes glaze over in fear. "How do you think Kieron found out? I ordered him to kill her, you know." Jaden's face turned red. The vein in his neck popped and he began screaming at her. He was ripping his throat raw as he cursed her name. Kaitlyn only seemed to be enjoying it.

"I can't stand the sight of you! You're repulsive!" He shouted. Suddenly, she was in front of Jaden. His voice cracked as he stopped talking immediately. She rested her two clawed fingers directly in front of his eyes.

"If you can't even look at me shall I help you out? Make it so that you never have to again?" After a moment of thick silence she cackled once again and dropped her hand, "That shut you up, huh? All of you men are the same. You can talk and talk," Kaitlyn then cast a glance over to Kieron, "But, when it comes down to it you're unbearably helpless." Jaden only grimaced at her, refusing to respond. She smirked and looked over his scythe once more. "I have to admit... you are quite talented. This is impressive for some junk dog like you." She smiled maliciously at the weapon then to Kieron. She slowly drifted over to him Kieron. "Move your hand." He did immediately, not hesitating. He knew if he hesitated she would bring him unimaginable pain. Just as he moved his hand aside she slammed the scythe back into place where it had been originally. He howled in agony and leaned back. He went to touch it. Slowly and gently brushing his fingers over the blade. She had jammed it deeper than it had been before.

"Why?!" Kieron growled. "I've gotten you everything yo-" Kaitlyn cut him off with a fierce look. He stopped speaking and stared up at her in torment. She only gave him an insane smile and turned to Jaden.

"I don't like an audience when I'm talking business." Jaden was frozen. He didn't move an inch as she walked around him. All Kieron saw was blood drip down to the hollow of his neck from behind, yet he knew what she was doing. Jaden clenched his jaw in pain as he tried desperately not to move. After she was done she sauntered around and twirled a bloody orange chip between her fingers as if it were a coin. "Now then. I won't be needing you anymore. Thank you for playing in my game. I'm sorry I have to disqualify you, but my pet failed to get your chip. He really did think you were Death himself." She giggled, "It was really quite amusing." With that, stalagmites at his temples slowly pushed into his head, blood spilling from the wounds as he screamed in terror and torture. Kaitlyn did not flinch as Jaden screamed her name in agony. She did not hesitate in killing Jaden and Kieron knew she would not hesitate in killing him either. "So then," she said nonchalantly as Jaden's body went limp, "what was it you were saying?"

Kieron could only stare in horror. This was why he wanted to have *Anastasis* ruled only by him. That was his original plan before he was confronted by Kaitlyn. She told him she knew exactly what his plan was, and that she didn't agree because she could show him something even greater. She told him that she had something that they could control. Something that would do whatever they wanted whenever they asked it. He was all for the idea until she told him the plan. He had tried to refuse, but then was met with intense torture that warped his mind forever. She had removed his chip and let him sit for three days. She let him slowly go insane and die. Then she had put it back. She repeated this until he realized she wouldn't stop until he joined her side. He was broken from his thoughts when he felt a sharp pain in his stomach. He reeled forward and the scythe dug deeper into his shoulder. He then vomited blood. She stood above him as he dry heaved.

"Don't make me repeat myself." Kaitlyn snarled, her voice changing from sweet to cold in a split second.

"I have everything you need. I have Arsen's chip and I was just going to get the other two after-"

"After getting Jaden's?" She finished for him. She raised a hand to her mouth and giggled. "That's cute... then please take your time. I love to watch this game so why not make it dramatic for me?" He nodded.

"It will be done..." Kieron answered, his head hung in defeat.

"Perfect." She purred with a smirk. "But, remember the two you have to get. It *must* be those two or else I can't do it. You wouldn't want me using your chip, right?"

"Okay... but-"

"No, no. Don't get second thoughts." She tapped her temple with her index finger. "I know exactly what you're thinking remember? Who kept you alive when Arsen impaled you? Who healed you whenever you took damage? Who has kept you in this game for this long, Kieron?"

"It's not-" She cut him off with a loud laugh. She ran a hand through her hair and slowly came to a stop. She gave him a cold look, her sharp features amplifying her irritated look. "It *is* a game, Kieron. It's *my* game. To be perfectly honest I could annihilate you right now. Just like last time. Then I can go and take what I want. I could do that so easily, but why don't I?" She leaned in close to him then. He craned his neck to look up at her, their faces centimeters apart. Her breath smelled like calming mint and her skin of lilacs. Kieron finally got a good look at her. She really was stunning. She looked just like a young woman. A harmless, beautiful young woman. Her eyes were a gorgeous jade green and her hair tumbled in perfect blonde curls that rested lightly on her shoulders. Her skin was flawless. It was perfectly smooth as she gripped his chin and made him stare at her. He didn't want to remember last time. The first time he met her and the last time he'd challenge her. But, she made him remember anyway. She made his brain replay exactly what had happened. He stared into her eyes and suddenly he felt the world around him waver then meld into the past.

He gasped for air and suddenly he was sitting at the meeting table in the center of the Atlantic. Everyone had left except him. He sat, twirling a pen between his fingers. Kaitlyn was there as well, staring out of the massive windows at the ocean. It was sunset and the orange-yellow light enveloped her. It was the first time he had met her. She was gorgeous and seemed so angelic, so pure. She turned to him then, and looked directly in his eyes. It was then that her maniacal smirk formed, and he remember how caught off guard he was. He remembered telling her of his plan and she had only giggled at him.

Then she had proceeded to tell him he could either side with her or die later on. That he could be a coward and tell the others about the plan she just spout to him, or he could feel true power.

"You're insane." He remembered telling her. Kaitlyn simply laughed. That crazy, maniacal laughter he didn't think could come from a woman.

"Am I? You really think so?" She teased. He didn't answer.

He couldn't think of a way to stop her except if he won in battle. He could convince her how bad of an idea this was. So he challenged her and lost horribly. He had died, but she healed him. He never understood how until she told him that she could manipulate anything with water. That the human body is 75% water and that she just reformed his flesh. When he didn't believe her she controlled him and made him stab himself against his will. Then she tortured him by taking out his chip. He remembered the pain as if he were feeling it all over again. He realized just how terrifying she was. She could make anyone do whatever she wanted against their will. She could open old wounds from scar tissue, she could freeze the blood in ones veins, and she could even replay memories in their mind. It was then that he gave her the name La Muerta. *She had only smirked of course and proceeded to tell him the phases of her plan. How she would hide in the shadows and be the puppeteer while he was the marionette. He never understood what she was thinking. He too could read minds, but every time he tried to read hers he would feel a head splitting pain that spread throughout his whole body as she gave him an amused look.*

When Kieron came to he was staring off into the distance, still on his knees. He looked down and saw a puddle of blood before him. Before he could ask, Kaitlyn answered his pending question. "You threw that up. It's quite funny really... how weak you actually are." He did not answer. He only stared up at the evil, fallen angel that stood a few steps away. In her hand were two chips. One was orange, and the other was gray. Jaden and Arsen's. "I know you kept it on you, but this belongs to me now. Also, about my plan; Ace, Gabriella and Isabel stay alive."

"I don't-" He tried.

"You don't have to understand." She cut him off, "Any other questions?"

"Could you remove this from my arm and heal it?" He requested, motioning towards Jaden's scythe that was still firmly planted in his arm. She grinned at him and walked over, running her hand along the handle of the scythe before ripping it out. He cried out in pain, his hand flying to where the wound should have been. It was completely healed over, but still ached tremendously. He muttered a thanks as he slowly stood, moving his shoulder in circles.

"Now then. Meet me at the Bunker when you're finished. And don't forget to make it interesting." She turned and walked past Jaden's body. Her steps were completely silent as she left and her *aura* disappeared within seconds.

***

Pharaoh Ace

Ace gaped in utter shock as Aurora's lifeless body dropped to the ground, the gaping hole in her chest flooding the ground beneath her with blood. Ace stared wide-eyed, his ears ringing from the loud noise. *What was that?* His question was answered immediately by the figure standing behind Aurora's lifeless body. He couldn't tell if it was a man or woman, but the figure was hooded with a bow and arrow slung over their shoulder. They were holding what looked to be a futuristic shotgun in the form of a hand held pistol. By the size of the barrel Ace could tell that it had to shoot at *least* twelve gage shells. The wound was too large to be a normal sized bullet and the shell was enormous. He heard Isabel scream a name. It wasn't Aurora's name, nor was it in despair. She shrieked Cicely's name furiously, causing the hooded figure and Ace to jump visibly.

"Cicely?" Ace questioned as he stared at Isabel. She only ignored him and drew her rapier. "Isabel be careful. She's got a gun." Isabel only gave him a look that obviously said "No, really?"

Isabel sped off towards the opponent. Large icicles erupted from the ground beneath the hooded figure. The assailant quickly jumped backward, dodging them fluently. Isabel was suddenly behind them, reaching out and grabbing ahold of their cloak. With one swift movement Isabel managed to tear the cloak off completely just as the assassin broke free. It *was* Cicely. Her golden eye patch glistening against the moonlight and sparkle of the light layer of snow. Her jaw was clenched as she glared at Isabel. Cicely only holstered the gun and fluidly readied a bow and arrow. The two watched each other carefully without moving an inch. Ace couldn't help but stare in shock as they both attacked at the same time. Just as Cicely let loose an arrow Isabel was sprinting towards her. Bella sliced the arrow in half, not pausing for even a second as she continued running. Cicely just continued to shoot arrow after arrow, keeping a perfect distance between them. Cicely jumped and let loose two arrows, both aimed for Isabel's stomach. Bella pivoted to the side just in time, or so he thought. The arrows changed course suddenly and grazed deeply into her armor. Ace took a step forward to help, but was quickly cut off by the sound of Gabriella's breathing.

He whipped around to find her sitting up. She was staring at Aurora's body then she looked to the fight going on. He was by her side in an instant, asking her if she was alright. She only rested her hand over his mouth to stop him from talking. He gazed at her as she slowly looked into his eyes.

"You don't understand what's actually going on, Ace. Kieron is collecting everyone's chips so he can put them in himself. He wants to be all powerful and take over *Anastasis*. He's going to kill us all... except me."

"Why only you?" Ace asked, his voice muffled from her hand. She gazed at him a moment and watched him. Her eyes showed she was scared, showed that she was unnerved somehow. She stiffened suddenly and her voice became a monotone.

"Because I agree with him. I'm going to help him become that powerful and then we can rule together." Ace stared in shock. She didn't really mean that did she?

"You... you're not serious."

She ran her fingers over his cheek and whispered, "I'm dead serious. You won't be able to stop him. No one will. He has a plan. A plan to take out the person he said is in charge of him. I don't know who that is, but I believe he will. I'll be sure to have him spare you for a little while." He couldn't believe his ears. He only stared dumbfounded as he felt his chest tighten. Ace started to shake his head, refusing to believe her. There's no way she would work for Kieron. She hated him... didn't she? "Ace, you should help us. Be a player on the winning side."

"Ace!" He heard Isabel call his name. He didn't understand why until he looked up. Isabel and Cicely were no longer in combat. Cicely's bow and arrow were thrown to the side and she held a long, double edged katana in hand. Isabel had her rapier shoved into the ground to lean on as she tore an arrow from her shoulder. "Ace. I need help, *now.*" Ace stared in confusion until he saw what she had meant. Kieron was walking towards them in a full body suit of gold and silver armor. He twirled his sword forward and it instantly burst into white flames. Ace glared and began to stand when he felt a sharp pain in his abdomen. He doubled over and coughed. Gabriella suddenly kicked out at him, nailing him in the temple. He cried out in pain as his head whipped to the side then smashed into the frozen ground.

Ace felt a fist in his hair as he was brought up to her face. He was so close he could feel her hot, labored breathing. Although his vision was still blurred, he couldn't see her hair covered face.

"Please don't look for me. I can't risk it." Her voice shook as she spoke and Ace could only stare. His mind was racing, trying desperately to figure out what she meant. "I have to go now. I have to go before he-" she paused then. It was only for a split second, but in that moment Ace knew exactly who to blame for this, "*I* shatter us." With that she pushed him away. Not with disgust, but as if she did not trust herself. She sprinted full speed towards Kieron. Isabel stepped in her way, but Gabriella was too fast. Gabriella whipped out one of her twin daggers as Isabel thrust her rapier forward. She quickly twirled and smashed her dagger into the rapier then, sliding beside Isabel, slammed her elbow into her side. Isabel lost balance momentarily, not enough to fall, but she did not have enough time to attack. Ace stared in shock as Gabriella came to a complete stop beside Kieron, who gave him a devilish smirk.

Ace's voice caught in his throat as he watched Kieron wrap an arm around Gabriella's side. He felt his heart lurch as the snake leaned close and whispered something in her ear. She did not respond as he did. Her eyes stared lifelessly in front of her. Kieron then turned her toward himself and lifted her chin. Ace felt a wave of rage envelope him. He clenched his jaw and balled his fists so tight his nails pricked his palms, blood seeping between his fingers. His mind went blank as he sprinted full speed for Kieron. He dove forward, hand blades first, aiming for his throat. He screamed Kieron's name feeling his throat being ripped raw. Kieron quickly sidestepped and gripped Ace's neck while he was in midair. Ace's eyes widened as he felt himself being flung backwards, landing on his back hard. He coughed and felt his head spin as he slowly tried to get up. He saw Isabel locked in fierce combat with Cicely again then saw the bottom of Kieron's boot as it slammed into his face. Ace cried out in pain as he was forced back down. He struggled against the heavy metal boot.

"She's mine now, *boy*. Too bad you couldn't steal her heart while you had the chance." Kieron taunted. Ace looked to Gabriella then, his eyes pleading with her to tell him it wasn't true. She only stood there. Her face was stone as she whipped out a dagger. He could not see Kieron, but he knew he had motioned to Aurora's body because Gabriella started to move towards it. She knelt beside it and removed the chip. Ace grit his teeth and felt tears start to form in his eyes as he watched helplessly. He stopped fighting back now, resting his arms by his sides. There was no use in fighting now. They had already won. Isabel continued to fight tooth and nail with Cicely, neither letting up as they received countless wounds from each other. Kieron had lifted his foot now and walked to Gabriella. She placed the chip in his hand and looked to Cicely.

"That's enough, Cicely!" Kieron bellowed. Cicely stopped and moved to Kieron's side.

"You really think *you* of all people can rule this place yourself? Be the sole king of *Anastasis*? You've broken so many laws, Kieron. Too many to count." Isabel growled at him.

"Have I though? If anything," Kieron stated as he stored the chip away and slammed his palm into Gabriella's back, pushing her forward towards Isabel, "*she* is a lawbreaker." Ace stared in shock as he slowly sat up. No one dared make a noise as Kieron smirked at them. "So is Ace. They broke one of the promises, 'no affairs between *Duces*'. I haven't broken any of those promises."

"Liar." Isabel spat, "You took over Cicely's territory-"

"I merely asked her for her land." He shrugged, cutting her off. "Isn't that right?" He asked looking to Cicely by his side. She nodded and grinned maliciously at Isabel.

"Cicely!" Isabel screeched.

Cicely grimaced and glared at Isabel, "What?" She spat.

"What is wrong with you? How could you side with him? How come you're so hostile toward me? Don't you remember the good times we've had? Why can't you tell me what I did?" Isabel pleaded, her voice cracking with every other word.

"What you did? What you did?!" Cicely barked a laugh, "You manipulative little-"

"I don't understand what I did to you! I-I really did cherish you... I told you that in *No Man's Land*. That's why I let you go." Isabel cut off, her eyes swelling with tears.

Cicely grit her teeth, "Cherish me? *Cherish me?!* You... you're the reason. You *abandoned* me! There was nothing you ever did? You're right, you didn't do anything to help when they did *this* to me." Cicely ripped her eyepatch off. Everyone went silent, even Kieron. Ace felt his stomach churn at the sight of Cicely's eye. The color was a dull, faded honey color. Her entire eye otherwise was a tattoo. It was a box with a line through it, but the outline was segmented. It surrounded her pupil and the veins in her eye had turned black from the ink. Ace glanced to Isabel, who was completely silent with her mouth agape. He could clearly see the emotions through her eyes. Her mask finally cracked.

"Cicely I-" Isabel tried.

"You seem to have finally remembered. Funny how you 'forgot', huh?"

"Well then seems you know the reason now right, Isabel?"

Isabel grit her teeth, "That's none of your concern."

"Well, tell me what else you have? Is there anything else I supposedly, hm? Anything that deserves retribution?" Kieron mused, a smug grin forming on his lips.

"You killed Arsen!" Ace yelled, his voice cracking, "I saw it with my own eyes!"

Kieron did not even glance in Ace's direction, "You're going to believe a criminal? You know you can't take any word that comes out of his mouth seriously since he lied about his little... affair. Actually, shouldn't *they* be in trouble?" Isabel was visibly shaking in anger, her knuckles whiter than the snow beneath them.

"You have no dirt on us Isabel. None." Cicely said amused.

"I just watched you kill Aurora. You're just as guilty." Ace said coldly. Cicely stiffened and looked to Kieron at first wide eyed before her eyes slowly narrowed. Kieron only smirked as he watched Isabel respond.

"Are you working with Cicely then? That would make you a partner in crime." Isabel said to Kieron with a glare.

All eyes were on him now as he ran a hand through his hair. Kieron studied her a moment before chuckling, "No, I'm not. She has been acting alone." Cicely glared daggers at him, then looked to Isabel. Before Cicely could speak Kieron was behind her. He slit her throat with his flamberge, blood pouring from her neck. Her mouth hung open as she fell forward and her *aura* dissipated for real this time. Isabel screamed her name and extended a hand out. Gabriella stood staring in shock, in fear as Kieron ripped the chip from Cicely's neck. Ace couldn't believe his eyes nor the words that Kieron had said after. "Now, that wasn't a crime either was it? She would have received the death penalty anyway, right?" He mused.

Ace was headed straight for Kieron, hand blades ready. He stopped inches from Kieron's neck when he heard his name called. Ace kept his eyes on Kieron, his lip curling up in detest.

"Ace don't. We can't touch him." He stared dumbfounded at her. He had killed so many people, and were letting him go? He watched as Kieron turned and smirked devilishly at him.

"You can keep the girl." He hissed as he walked past, brushing against Ace as he went. Ace felt his entire body shaking with rage as the snake walked off into the distance. Isabel went off to stop the soldiers from fighting after picking up the gun that Cicely had. Suddenly, Gabriella stepped in front of Ace.

"Ace..." He heard her whisper. He didn't answer. He couldn't look at her. "Ace, I couldn't control my body."

"Liar." Ace mumbled as he stared at the ground, "Why don't you just go off with him since you're involved with him like that?"

"Ace don't be ridiculous. Me and Isabel had this-" She tried.

"Just shut up." His voice was like a razor, cutting her off maliciously. "It'll never be me will it?" She stared at him silently. She reached for his hand, whispering his name quietly. He took a step back. He couldn't wrap his head around all that had just happened, so he walked around her. He ignored her as she called his name, but she didn't follow him. Ace brushed past Isabel on his way back to Arsen's castle. He sped off and, when he was out of sight, took a quick turn toward the Atlantic. He knew Isabel and Gabriella would not see him if he cut across the ocean to follow Kieron's *aura*.

If they won't help me, he thought as he tucked Cicely's gun deeper into his armor, *I'll stop him myself.*

Chapter 23: *The Truth*

Year 3062

The Scientist burst into the Boss's study, his glasses unaligned and his hair a mess. His lab coat was in disarray. A sleeve was ripped off and his arm was bleeding. He was breathing heavily as he leaned his back against the large metal door that led into the massive lab from which he came. His eyes were wide and wild. There was loud yelling and crashing that could be heard in the room behind him.

"Sir! Sir, we have a big problem!" The Scientist cried out.

The Boss sat in a luxurious chair behind a large, polished wood desk. Holo screens were lit up in front of him with various important documents. One of the documents he was filling out was a form on the experiments in the room behind The Scientist. It had the Subjects in numerical order, but no names were attached. There was only a picture of their face and their powers that the chip had given them. The Scientist was still rambling on about how his coworkers were fighting and killing each other over some argument. The Boss held up a hand and The Scientist stopped speaking immediately. "Is Subject Nine acting up again?" The Boss sighed irritably.

"No sir, Arse- I mean, Subject Nine has not spoken since we implanted the chip. In fact, all of the Subjects are heavily intoxicated with anesthesia, and shouldn't be awake at all until tomorrow morning at the least."

"Then what is it?" The Boss questioned.

"It's Subject Three again sir... *It* caused the fights and deaths of a few other scientists."

The Boss sat up straight and stared at the shaking worker before him, "How?"

"I-I don't know sir. Maybe we shouldn't have given any of the Subjects telekinesis at all. I believe *It* read the minds of all of us or listened to our conversations in the lab. *It* waited until all the other Subjects would be heavily sedated. For some reason the anesthesia isn't effecting *It* as much as the others. *It* had to have waited at least a few months, but why spring this now? For fun? That's right *It had* to have waited. *It* must have because *It* called one of us over and said something... I don't know what *It* said, but it was enough to cause them all to riot. I had just walked in and they were at each other's throats. I don't know what to do, Boss. What do we do?"

"Put Subject Three in solitary confinement after you fix the lab. As for the others, either make them stop fighting yourself or call the police." The Boss answered.

"But I-" The Scientist tried.

"I'm busy."

"Of course, sir." The Scientist nodded. He quickly tapped on his wrist, a holographic screen popping up.

"Oh also," The boss said slowly as he stared at the names on the Holo screen, "About their tattoos... make sure Subject Three has one that is an indication to *It's* personality in some way."

"Yes, sir." The Scientist nodded once again before sifting through applications on the Holo. He switched to the holographic and entered "911" hastily, "How about endurance? Since *It* waited so long just to cause a small bit of chaos?"

The Boss's eyes lit up as he muttered, "perfect". He began typing up the meanings of the tattoos and putting the pictures next to each Subject's number. The Scientist opened up the large metal door and the crashing and yelling became even louder. The Boss grit his teeth and glanced up out the door. He made direct eye contact with Subject Three, who stared back at him smiling. It was a crazy sort of smile. The kind of smile that only maniacs have. It sent a chill through him, but he couldn't look away. There was blood splashed on *It's* scrubs and part of *It's* face. He then heard *It's* voice echo in his mind. It sounded similar to that of nails on a chalkboard to him; "*Endurance... very nice. To play a game correctly you must have endurance. Isn't that right,* Dad?"

***

Pharaoh Ace

The Pharaoh skimmed across the Atlantic in seconds, following Kieron's *aura*. He came to a sudden stop on the shore of *No Man's Land*.

He's in Isabel's territory? Why? Ace thought to himself. Of course. It's to expand his land, that's why. Ace growled in frustration and hurried across to the border and toward the town square of Eagle Territory. No way was he going to let Kieron take over here too. He was going to get revenge no matter what the consequences were. Ace then saw Kieron walk into the town square where a body lay in a large pool of blood. Jaden. Ace had wondered why he hadn't felt his *aura* in a while, but he thought it was because he was laying low so that Kieron wouldn't know where he was. Kieron was truly a monster. An evil, insane monster. However, Ace stayed put and watched Kieron look to Isabel's castle instead of going after him. Kieron was just sitting there staring into the dark shadows that covered the pathway up to the massive palace. *What is he staring at?* Ace wondered. It was then that Kieron slowly turned and looked directly at Ace.

"Come on out boy and fight me like you came to. I'm not holding back anymore." Kieron's voice boomed. Ace was suddenly in front of him, thrusting his hand blades forward to Kieron's stomach. Kieron sidestepped them just in time and kicked out at Ace, connecting with his side. Ace went flying in the opposite direction. He managed to land on his feet and skid to a stop.

"How did you know I was here?" Ace asked, his fists clenched. "I didn't make a sound."

"You honestly don't need to know. It's too late... everything is over now. All went according to plan and there is nothing we can do to stop it. It's all over."

Ace stared, confused, "*We?* What do you mean?"

Kieron watched him carefully a moment, but did not answer. Ace felt his blood boil and suddenly whipped out Cicely's gun, pointing it directly at Kieron. "Answer me!" Ace yelled, his hand shaking.

"You won't shoot me. Telling you everything now would be a waste of time since you'll find out very soon anyway." Kieron said in monotone.

"I *will* shoot you! I came here to kill you! What makes you think I won't shoot you?! Tell me everything right now!" Ace hollered, his hand trembling.

"Go ahead and shoot me then! Come on!" Kieron roared back, opening his arms wide. He then started to laugh while staring directly into Ace's eyes. "We're going to die soon anyway. When *La Muerta* gets here we're all going to die." Ace had so many questions, but he felt his mind go blank. Anger consumed him and the only thing that woke him back up was the loud crack of a gunshot. His eyes widened as time seemed to slow. The gun whipped his arm backward from the recoil, and the giant bullet was headed straight for Kieron's chest. He watched in horror as it go closer and closer. Then it hit him.

Ace gaped as the bullet passed right through Kieron's body and into the wall behind him. Kieron's face was one of shock as well. No, not shock. That was *fear.* Someone was here now. Someone other than them, but he couldn't place the *aura*. Ace went to turn his head, but it wouldn't move. He was suddenly in front of Kieron, his hand blade inches from the snake's throat. Kieron did not move as blood trickled down his neck from the slight pressure of Ace's weapon. Ace felt his chest tighten in terror as he tried to move his body. He was no longer in control of his actions or able to move any part of his body for that matter. *How is this happening? Why can't I control my body?* He thought to himself. Kieron seemed unable to move either. He only stared blankly behind Ace.

"How cute. You brought a friend, Kieron." A voice said from behind Ace. The voice was muffled as if he was underwater. He couldn't tell whether the person behind him was male or female. Kieron's face was a look of panic. It was as if he was in his worst nightmare. "No matter. I'm glad you brought him of all people. Isabel is sure to follow now. Then we can really start the party." The person behind Ace slowly traced the back of his neck. He felt the sharp coolness of metal outline the area of his chip. Ace felt shivers run down his spine. He quivered and swallowed hard at the lump in his throat.

No... please don't, He begged, *please don't take it.*

"Oh, I won't. I still want you in my game." The voice purred in his ear. "You're a vital piece I need, so I won't kill you." Ace felt his body shift out of the way, but he was still staring straight ahead. Kieron was just barley in his peripherals. The snake's body was still frozen in place as the person behind Ace moved closer. Ace only saw a flash of blood and heard Kieron's muffled scream. Ace flinched as a spray of blood came into view. "I guess it really doesn't matter if you know who I am then, Ace." The voice spoke, becoming more and more identifiable. This person was definitely female, but who? "Allow me to formally introduce myself, since we haven't officially met yet. In fact, I don't believe we've even spoken to each other besides the greeting you gave me at your party." She said as she slowly walked into view.

"Kaitlyn?" Ace asked, dumbfounded. "What... I don't under-" Ace stopped himself when he saw what was in her hand. She had five computer chips in between each finger, each one a different color. Ace knew exactly who's they were just by the color. Kieron's was a dark red, Jaden's was orange, Cicely's was black, Aurora's was purple, and a final gray chip. *Arsen's*. Ace felt his chest tighten at the sight. He wanted to scream. To ask her why she was holding them. She had never made herself noticeable. She was always sticking to the background. *But, why?* He thought to himself.

"Why? Because, It's all been a part of my plan. Even since the very beginning. Soon Isabel will show up, having seen you run off. She may or may not bring Gabriella, either way doesn't matter much." Kaitlyn explained as she examined each of the chips, "Then I will go into the Bunker and show you what I plan to do."

"Was killing Arsen part of your plan, you sick freak?" Ace snapped, glowering at her. He could feel his heart pounding and rise to his throat as she giggled.

Kaitlyn smiled, a wicked sort of smile, as she spoke, "Oh no. Not at all. You see, Ace, I never planned on having your brother killed. In fact, he had a pretty crucial role. Kieron made that decision himself. Would you like to know why?" Kaitlyn questioned as she held up Arsen's chip in front of Ace. Ace stared at it and bit back his emotions. He felt tears well up in his eyes as he refused to answer. Kaitlyn leaned in close and whispered, "Two reasons... revenge, and because he is a *megalomaniac*."

"Did you kill him? Did you kill the *megalomaniac*?" Ace asked, his voice shaking.

"Oh, no. That wouldn't be any fun. See, you're going to have to team up with him if you want to stop my plans. But, I might as well explain everything when Isabel gets here with your lover. I don't feel like repeating myself." She answered, looking up at Isabel's castle.

"I'll never work with him. *Never*. He-" Ace tried.

"We all know what he's done to you, Ace. Killed your brother, took Gabriella's heart, and stole any chance of happiness on this God forsaken planet, right?" Kaitlyn grinned at him as he sucked in a breath, "Still stings doesn't it? Knowing the one you love chose a maniac over you. Chose the man that murdered your brother in cold blood. You know Ace... you can still switch sides. You won't have to work with him. You can leave him to die right now. He'll be dead in three days anyway. You have no one left to fight for, Ace. So, why not help me rule *Anastasias* and be a winner in this game too?" Her voice was like silk as she spoke close to his ear. It sounded so right to Ace just then. Nothing else mattered anymore, so why not?

Before he could answer there was a sudden blow to the back of Ace's head. His vision get blurred as he fell forward onto the ground. Kaitlyn's voice sounded sweet as everything went black, "Don't sleep for too long."

Ace did not dream of anything while he was unconscious. It was completely dark and silent in his mind. He didn't know anything. He didn't feel anything. It was like he didn't exist. Suddenly, he felt a damp coolness on his cheek. *What is that?* He groaned, a pain in his neck starting to throb. *Where am I?* His eyes slowly fluttered open. How long had he been unconscious? His eyes met Kieron's. His brother's killer was in a heap still, but dried blood coated his body. He was pale and visibly shaking. He heard Kaitlyn's voice, snapping him back to reality. His memories flooded back and he quickly sat up with a gasp.

"Good morning, sleeping beauty." She was crouched in front of him. She smiled warmly at him. Did all of that actually happen? Kaitlyn isn't the bad guy right? "If you're wondering, you've been out for a while... a day or so at the least. I put Kieron's chip back in and took it out a few minutes ago, so he won't die just yet." Her voice, appearances and smile clashed with her words. How can someone who looks like that be like *this?*

"What happened?"

"Oh, nothing much... I was just playing with Kieron while you were napping." She answered playfully, "But, who cares about him anyway? What I *really* wanna know is if you've decided to be on my team or not?"

"No. Don't... listen." Kieron spoke from the ground. Ace couldn't see him, but he sounded as if he was in immense pain. "She'll just drop you as soon as... she gets what she wants. *Don't do it.*" It almost sounded as if he was pleading.

"Why do you care anyway?" Ace retorted, clenching his fists. "You took *everything* from me." He slammed his fist onto the cobbleston as he rose to his knees. The ground quaked under his fist, blood forming on his hand. He slowly stood up. *I can move again?* He thought. He looked down at Kieron. His entire back was torn open, as well as the back of his neck. He was on the ground, unable to move. Ace could only stare a moment before looking to Kaitlyn. He realized that he felt nothing for Kieron. He did not feel pity, only anger and loathing. Kaitlyn was not looking at Ace anymore. She smirked and raised a finger to her lips.

"Hush now children. Our guests have arrived." Kaitlyn said in a mocking tone. Ace whipped around to see Isabel and Gabriella. He felt his heart drop as he saw Gabriella face contort with so many different emotions at once.

"Kaitlyn!?" Gabriella and Isabel asked in unison, both with expressions of utter shock.

"I'm glad you all could make it." Kaitlyn mused as she gently placed Arsen's chip in Ace's hand. Ace stared at it a moment then looked at Kaitlyn one last time. "That chip belongs to you, just as these," she held up the remaining four chips, "belong to me."

"Why do you need them? What are you planning, Kaitlyn? What exactly do you gain?" Isabel challenged, watching Kaitlyn intently.

"Well, allow me to explain now that all the players are here. I'm sure almost none of you remember, but back when the experiments took place I was given my powers. Water and telekinesis. Because of this, I was able to deter most of the anesthesia given to me. I made a bit of a mess and for that I was sent to solitary confinement. That's where I was contacted by the 'enemy'. Don't ask me how, because I still don't know to this day. But, they told me I could gain unimaginable power by capturing all of the chips and placing them in my own slots. However, I do not require immense amounts of power. What I desire most, what I enjoy seeing the most, is chaos. Chaos is exciting. It's *fun*. The enemy-the HEB's-soon came to realize this. So, they told me that inside the Bunker would be a special console in which I could communicate with *their* last resort." Ace, as well as everyone else, stared in confusion as she spoke.

"The cyborgs... the things that the humans fought hundreds of years ago? The reason why we're here? *Those HEB's*?" Gabriella asked. Her voice was so perfect it made Ace retch. He couldn't stand hearing her voice anymore.

"Correct." Kaitlyn answered, "The *HEB's* that mankind had created. The cyborgs that turned around and started a war. They contacted me. It's foolish really, that the greatest human minds could not see that the *HEB's* would make their own second chance as well." Kaitlyn watched Ace a moment, her eyes peering directly through his mind. "Now, Ace," she purred as she stepped closer to him, her lips next to his ear, "you'll help me, right? These *HEB's*... they can bring your brother back." Ace felt his eyes widen at her words. *Bring Arsen back?*

"Ace, don't listen to her!" Isabel cried out. Ace felt his mind swimming. Bring Arsen back, or stop whatever Kaitlyn had planned. He felt his head begin to ache as he struggled to think. Arsen could come back. He could be with him again. He didn't know how Kaitlyn planned to bring him back, or if she even would for that matter... but was that method worth it?

No. Arsen is worth it. Arsen is worth everything. He thought to himself.

"Ace." Gabriella's voice severed his thoughts like a knife. Ace's head whipped up to face her and made direct eye contact. "I know you won't believe me... but, I need you to know that I was never against you. I promise you. So please consider this realistically. What does Kaitlyn really want from you? How do you know that whatever she promised you is even possible? Even if it is, how does-"

"I benefit from this because it makes my job much easier." Kaitlyn cut in harshly. She glared daggers at Gabriella as she spoke.

"What do you even gain from bringing the enemy that demolished the human race back into existence?" Isabel retorted, taking a step forward.

Kaitlyn only smirked as she tilted her head to the side. Her smile only widening as she answered, "Why? Because I thrive for *chaos*. I can't even begin to explain to you how much I *adore* it. Watching chaos unfold and seeing absolute destruction... doesn't it just sound *marvelous*?! Observing humanity reduced to ashes over and over again by its own self-destruction is the most fascinating thing, don't you think?"

Ace stared in shock at Kaitlyn. There was no way a person worse than Kieron could exist, yet here she stood. Kaitlyn had no goal. She only wanted to watch the world be incinerated in some form. It was terrifying,

"Ace, you can't seriously be contemplating this. Are you really going to side with *her?"* Gabriella asked, her voice taunt.

Ace felt his chest constrict. He ground his teeth and looked to the ground a moment before mustering the courage. He lifted his head and gazed directly into Gabriella's eyes. He couldn't let any other thoughts into his mind or everything that's happened would be for nothing. He had to put on a mask, in his mind, his emotions and his thoughts. "I'm going to help Kaitlyn." He replied to Gabriella, his voice in monotone. Isabel, Gabriella and Kieron-who had been silent the entire time-all gaped at him in shock. All except Kaitlyn. Kaitlyn was the only one that was not surprised by his answer. As Ace looked to her he saw the wheels in her head turning.

"Why?" Gabriella questioned. Her tone was hard and demanding. As if she didn't believe him.

Stop. He thought.

"Why, Ace?" Her voice insistent. Just Gabriella saying his name made his already pounding heart skip a beat. Gabriella's hands were in fists at her sides. She was standing tall as she spoke, "Why do you suddenly support the bad guy? If it's because of Arsen-"

"It's not." Ace lied, cutting her off. "It's because... it just sounds *exhilarating* doesn't it? It's not like you'll need me anymore anyway, you've got Kieron." His tone suddenly acidic.

"Gabriella did what she had to do to get inside, Ace." Isabel snapped. "In no way was she ever against us. You should know better than anyone that she was trying to protect us."

"He loves you, you know." Ace told. He was surprised at how cold he sounded, but the words just bubbled up. They came from deep inside his stomach and spewed out. "Kieron, I mean. He loves you, Gabriella. I see the way he looks at you. The way he... the way he spoke to you. I know you better than anyone here, so I know you don't love anyone. I know that you stopped believing love existed, because you've never felt that strongly for anyone before. The only person you came close to loving is Arsen. I understand that you... that you won't let me in because of that. Maybe it's because I'm not good enough, but maybe you can find someone who loves you just as much as I do. Someone that can make you happy. That's all I want. No, that's all I wanted." Ace raised his head to look at Gabriella, their eyes locking immediately. He felt all eyes on him as he spoke, but he felt like it was just Gabriella and himself at the moment. His heart felt like it was being squeezed as he vomited his feelings in the form of words. "It's different now. What I want now is the one person who truly cared about me. The only person that actually loved me because right now there is no one left alive who does. Even if it means destroying the human race again, I am going to get my brother back." Ace clenched his teeth as he felt a tear roll down his cheek, which mimicking the one that rolled down Gabriella's. Had he made her cry? Or was she only worried about her own life in danger? It didn't matter anymore. The feelings weren't mutual.

"Ace I-" Gabriella tried, her voice shaking.

"How did you know?" Kieron asked, struggling to his knees.

Ace did not answer. He only looked to Kaitlyn for confirmation. She was grinning a maniacal smile that sent chills down his back. Ace began to turn his head to look to Isabel and Gabriella again when he felt a hand grip his chin. His eyes widened as Kaitlyn forced him to face her. "Want to see something interesting?" She breathed close to his face. He could only stare in shock as she leaned in and kissed him. Their lips brushing briefly before pressing together. It was drawn out and slow, but not the same as Gabriella. He felt nothing, only the odd coldness of Kaitlyn's mouth. She slowly pulled away with a smirk. Ace felt his cheeks flush as he slowly turned his head to Gabriella. She was stood staring in utter shock, as was Isabel and Kieron. However, Gabriella's expression was slightly different. It was one that was in pain, no... agony. Ace couldn't understand why or what she was feeling at all.

Why? Why is she upset by that? He thought to himself, unable to look away from Gabriella. He felt Kaitlyn's lips close to his ear as she whispered; "I wonder... why would she be so upset if she doesn't love you, Ace? Isn't that strange?"

"Now then, since I've had my fun with this love triangle," Kaitlyn said aloud as she moved away from Ace and turned on her heel to walk towards the Bunker, "I think it's about time I started up round two."

Isabel unsheathed her rapier as she spoke, "I can't let you do that, Kaitlyn."

"Oh, and Ace," Kaitlyn stated as she held up Arsen's chip in one hand, "I'll give you what's rightfully yours if you help me out." *How did she-* Ace patted himself down for the chip before he shook the thoughts from his head and stared at Kaitlyn as she continued to walk away. He hesitated as Isabel sped past him, sweat beads forming on his temple. Suddenly, Ace was in front of Isabel. He slammed his palm into her stomach, sending her flying backwards towards Gabriella.

"Ace!" Gabriella cried out. She was suddenly sprinting for him, both knives drawn. Instantly she was beside him and throwing a right hook with her blade. Ace ducked just in time to avoid it. He spun on his heel, still crouched, in a circle and managed to connect with her feet. Gabriella fell to the side and landed harshly. Ace looked up to see Isabel sprinting full force towards the pathway to her castle. He took off after her as fast as he could, but was stopped almost immediately. He felt his head snap backwards from Gabriella's arm as she clotheslined him, his head bouncing off of her then off of the walkway. His hand flew to his face as blood poured out of his nose.

How do you even fight teleportation? Ace thought. He lifted his head and managed to see Isabel close to the exit of the town square. He raised his hand swiftly and a massive wall of concrete formed, cutting off her only route to the castle.

"Gabriella! Keep him occupied while I take down this wall!" Isabel shouted as she began blasting the wall with water and ice. Chips of concrete and stone fell in piles as Isabel slowly worked on creating a hole. Ace stood up only to be knocked down again by Gabriella's foot. She pinned him to the ground, her boot firmly pressing him down.

"Please... I'm trusting you, Ace. I'm trusting you have a plan and you aren't going to just let us all die." She said quietly to him, slowly taking her foot off of his chest. Ace stayed put on the ground, watching her. He analyzed every inch of her face. The curve of her mouth and the shimmer in her eyes from the fountain beside them. It was then that he realized how much he adored her. "I'm serious you idiot. If you... if you don't fix this, Ace I swear. I'll seriously hate you forever." She said, her voice shaking. He couldn't help but gape at her. She was beautiful even when she cried. Even in her prideful way of weeping she was absolutely gorgeous. Her shoulders never shook and there was no way to tell she was shedding tear after tear.

"Gabriella... I need to get Arsen back." Ace responded shortly, not letting up his mask for even a moment. He managed to steal a glance at his wall that Isabel was attempting to tear down. She was halfway through now and Ace slowly closed his eyes and relaxed. He bought enough time. He was done fighting, for now.

Chapter 24: *Clavis Regni*

Queen Kaitlyn

Kaitlyn couldn't help but bite her lip in excitement as she neared the Bunker. It's massiveness still took her by surprise as she neared it. It was to the right of Isabel's castle, just before the entrance. The stark whiteness of it now dulled by the years of being unused. It had dirt and grass stains all over and the door was firmly shut. As Kaitlyn walked she held up the five *Duces* chips. She placed the gray one, Arsen's, back into her armor and kept the others out. As she neared the Bunker, she looked back towards the town square only to see Ace fending off both Gabriella and Isabel. Kaitlyn then opened the door to the Bunker. It let out a loud and long hiss before letting up. She swung it open and stepped inside, the interior bathed in a red flashing light. She slowly walked down the narrow hallway past entrances to thousands of different rooms as she made her way to the control room. Kaitlyn ran her hand along the walls and closed doors of the many dorms before stopping at number 133. She pushed the door open and glanced inside. The room was entirely bare, unlike the other rooms that had some kind of decoration still left inside or a different arrangement of the given necessities. *Memories...* She felt a small grin creep onto her face as she continued walking. She could faintly hear the distant fighting as well as the sound of the beeping and clicking coming from the control panel up ahead.

"The four elements go in the corresponding places." Kaitlyn recited to herself as she approached the immense, high tech control panel. The control panel was the width of the room. On the surface were thousands of different buttons, switches and levers, as well as holographic keyboards with numbers and symbols she didn't recognize. Kaitlyn felt underneath the panel and flipped the switch, causing Holo screens to pop up all around her. She scanned all of them until she found the hidden folder labeled "*Clavis Regni*" and tapped it. When it opened up, a required key code bar flashed on screen in red. She smirked to herself as she looked to the symbols on the holographic keypad that lay on the control panel. She quickly entered "*Anastasis*" and watched as the control panel itself split apart to reveal four chip placements. Above each slot was a symbol for water, fire, earth, and wind. She placed each chip in it's corresponding slot. Aurora's purple chip into the water slot, Kieron's red chip in the fire slot, Jaden's orange chip in the earth slot, and Cicely's black chip in the wind slot.

Kaitlyn took a step back as the chips sunk into the control panel. The entire panel lit up stark red, flooding the room in a dark crimson color. It then began beeping. It sounded like an alarm, the bleeping echoing loudly as all of the Holo screens faded away. A singular wall width screen suddenly burst into view directly in front of her with a timer counting down.

"Three minutes." Kaitlyn said aloud with a half-smile. She quickly turned and raced out of the Bunker, emerging outside just as the Bunker was swallowed up into the depths of the Earth.

***

Pharaoh Ace

Ace slowly sat up as Isabel burst through the massive wall he had constructed. Scattered pieces of debris lay all around the large opening she had created. Isabel turned her head towards Ace and Gabriella and began to say Gabriella's name.

"Isaaa-*bell*." Kaitlyn sang, cutting her off before she could speak. Isabel's eyes widened as she slowly started to turn her head to the wall where the voice was coming from. Ace could only watch, helpless beside Gabriella, as Kaitlyn appeared from the opening at a full sprint. Time slowed as Kaitlyn thrust her clawed mesh gauntlet into Isabel's stomach at top speed, sending her hurtling backwards and into the large fountain. She landed harshly on her back, and Ace was sure he saw blood erupt from her mouth.

"Ace," Kaitlyn's voice startled him as he quickly looked to her, "your brother's chip, as promised for being my little helper." She held up a gray chip. Ace quickly pushed himself up off of the ground to stand, which threw Gabriella off balance. He sprinted over and was suddenly beside her. Kaitlyn gently placed in in his hands and smirked. "I hope you'll forgive me."

"Wh-" Ace was cut off by an ear splitting screech that was seemingly coming from everywhere and nowhere at once. Ace quickly covered his ears trying to block out the noise. The sound only getting louder as it seemed to get closer. He looked up and saw a bright red and orange glow. He couldn't tell exactly what it was, only that it was on fire and falling incredibly fast. The screech was now a roar as it made it's descent, landing on the other side of the town square and cratered the ground beneath it. Ace could only stare in shock. It looked like a futuristic coffin. It was oddly shaped and firmly planted in the ground. There was no handle, only a small circular window towards the top that looked to be frozen over. He couldn't see what was inside, but he felt that whatever was inside was extremely bad. He felt the hairs on the back of his neck stand on end as the coffin-like object let out a loud hiss and steam flushed out of the sides. Ace swiftly looked to Gabriella and was suddenly in front of her. He hastily surveyed the area, spotting Isabel now sitting up beside the fountain. Her hair was matted down and soaked by the water, as well as the rest of her. Her face was stark white and her eyes locked on the futuristic coffin. Ace then looked to see Kieron, he was still on the ground, but staring in shock at the coffin as well. The Pharaoh did not have to look to know that Kaitlyn was smiling.

The coffin then buzzed before the front receded into the side of the coffin with a hiss, allowing them to see what would emerge. Inside was what looked like a robot of sorts. Sleek metal on it's shoulders and parts of its legs and head. It clanked as it slowly moved out of the tomb that had been holding it. It's feet sank into the stone as it emerged. Ace could see it better now. It had to be at least seven feet tall, and looked very human-like. The abdomen of the cyborg held multiple gears and gadgets that Ace didn't recognize. It looked extremely advanced in technology, but grotesquely so. He could see the insides working and moving as if it were actually *alive*. It did not have much of a face either. Only a single eye in the center of its forehead. There was no mouth or nose. It's entire face looked like a mask. Tubes and wires curved out of the back and sides of it's neck as it slowly stood tall. It then *whirred* and *clicked* as its singular eye lit up a deep blue and scanned the area.

"Location; Anastasis. *Four unknown subjects identified."* A deep, gravelly voice spoke. Ace stared in awe and fear as it looked to each one of them. The cyborg *chattered, whirred* and *clicked* after each sentence it said. *"Subjects identified as human's* 'Last Resort'. *Subjects One, Two, Three, Seven, and Five present. Will negotiate."*

No one dared speak as it took a few steps forward then looked up towards Isabel's castle and then back at each of them. Ace watched as it spoke again in it's low, penetrating voice. *"Experiments,"* Ace grit his teeth at the word, *"I am known as* Victorum. *You are creations of the humans, known as their 'last resort'. For too long the human race has made mistakes. This planet is nearing devastation beyond repair. Survival is miniscule. I offer you a choice; immediate termination, or a qualification test." Why is everything a "choose this or die" question?* Ace thought to himself irritably.

"We'll take the qualification test." Kaitlyn replied confidently. The rest of the *Duces* looked to her with wide eyes.

"Salvation to a superior existence is reserved to those who survive. Qualification test initiated." The cyborg droned. Ace swallowed hard at the lump in his throat as the robots chest lit up a light blue. The *whirring* and *clicking* sounds began to get louder. *"Which experiment will be tested first?"*

"I will." Kaitlyn said as she stepped forward with a grin.

"Subject Three. Chip upgrades indicate water elemental and telekinetic powers including; telepathy, gravity manipulation and minor teleportation." The cyborg paused

a moment before continuing with a *chattering* sound. *"Strength noted as well. Test initiating."*

Kaitlyn tightened her clawed, mesh looking glove as she prepared herself. The cyborg stood straight. The light in its eye and chest suddenly turned red. Ace stepped back, pushing Gabriella backwards and away from the center of the town square. He saw Isabel quickly grab and move Kieron and herself off to the side as well. Kaitlyn was suddenly in front of the cyborg. Ace hadn't even seen her move toward it. Kaitlyn's clawed hand was caught by Victorum's massive metallic hand, seconds from what looked to be the *HEB's* "heart". Kaitlyn was thrown backwards at lightning speed and force. She managed to land on her feet on the other side of the town square. The cyborg began walking towards her silently. It's body standing perfectly straight. Ace did not hear it *whirr* or *click* anymore only dead silence.

Kaitlyn began sprinting towards the cyborg with an unnerving smile. It happens within seconds. Icicles erupted from the ground all around the *HEB*. Just as they were about to make contact it ducked and whipped it's hand out, grabbing Kaitlyn firmly around the waist just as she got close enough. Kaitlyn's body was immediately flung upwards into the air. Ace gaped as the cyborg jumped and shattered the ice above it. It was directly in front of Kaitlyn now, both of them suspended in the air for a moment. Kaitlyn stared in shock as she was roundhouse kicked in midair, and sent hurtling backward into a building just above Ace and Gabriella. Debris and dust flooded out and around her, raining down on Ace and Gabriella as well, as she cratered the structure. The Cyborg landed gracefully and stood slowly as it gazed off to where Kaitlyn had landed. Suddenly, she was immediately in front of it without a scratch on her. Time slowed and Ace could only watch as the robot moved in slow motion to grip her head while Kaitlyn moved in a blur of motion. The cyborg stopped its movement immediately and its colors changed back to blue as Kaitlyn's hand made contact with the circular object in its chest.

"Subject Three has passed phase one. Commencing phase two." The cyborgs booming voice announced. Kaitlyn's eyes suddenly widened as she watched the cyborgs chest light up red again. Ace stared in confusion as her *aura* dissipated, and she began moving slower. The cyborg would throw punches and kicks at an inhumane speed while Kaitlyn just barely dodged them. However, she quickly regained her composure and began to fight back. Matching the robots speed, Kaitlyn began landing blow after blow on the machine. The cyborg dodged an incoming attack from Kaitlyn's clawed hand, moving its head to the side just in time. Then it punched her in the stomach and sent her flying backward, skidding along the ground.

What is going on? Why isn't she using her elemental or telekinesis? He thought to himself.

"That thing shut off her chip." Gabriella said in awe. He looked to her and watched her a moment.

"How do you know?" Ace asked.

"Because, she'd still be using it right now if it hadn't."

Ace turned back to the fight. Kaitlyn now had a crescent halberd in hand and there was blood seeping from her hairline, yet she was smiling as she fought. She was merciless, aiming for the sphere in it's chest as if it were it's heart. Her eyes told everything. They were the eyes of someone whose only instinct is to kill and destroy. She fluidly swung the halberd and managed to scratch the cyborg almost every time. The robot only continued to try and swing at her, stopping her millimeters from it's core each time she came close. Just then, Kaitlyn jumped backward and reeled her arm back, holding her weapon like a spear. She grinned as she threw it with unreasonable accuracy, aiming for its chest. The robot caught it just before it had made contact, but it's attention was misplaced. While it was looking at the halberd it had not noticed Kaitlyn jump up and land gracefully on the handle of her weapon. She quickly took two steps and drop kicked the cyborgs head. The *HEB's* head pitched backward unnaturally as it staggered backward. It was then that Kaitlyn attacked, thrusting her arm forward and touching the circular object in the machines chest. Instantly, the robot turned back to it's original blue color. It *whirred* then *chattered* as it's head moved back into place to look down at Kaitlyn.

"Subject Three has passed phase two. Initiating phase three; final phase."

"Finally." Kaitlyn said aloud, moving backward and away as the cyborg's usual noises became louder. The chest lit up and it's eye turned red once more. The machine stared at Kaitlyn, her halberd still in it's hand. Then it suddenly incinerated it, the flames licking up it's arm and hand. Kaitlyn frowned in irritation before rushing the machine, her clawed hand ready. She propelled herself forward toward it's chest, but was stopped short as the machine moved to the side and gripped her arm with uncanny speed. Kaitlyn howled in pain as it squeezed down and ripped the glove off. Ace then saw her tattoo, and recognized it immediately.

"Endurance..." He whispered to himself. Gabriella asked him what he meant, but he only ignored her. He couldn't take his eyes away for a second. Kaitlyn's cursing was cut off by the cyborg's next attack. It swung her body like a rag doll onto the ground. Ace winced as her back arched and blood sprayed from her mouth once she made contact. A crater formed below her from the impact and Ace was surprised as he watched her slowly get up. The robot kicked out at her, but Kaitlyn quickly rolled to the side and managed to get up on her feet.

"Hand to hand it is." She said grimacing in pain. Ace was astounded at how she could still move so fluently. She dodged each on coming attack, diving and spinning out of the way. The machine punched out at her then, just missing her. She used it's arm as leverage and kicked out at it's face. The cyborg's head snapping freakishly to the side with each kick. It went to grab her, but missed as she swung underneath and planted a firm two foot kick on the side of it's knee. The robot lost balance momentarily, but it was enough time for her to slide underneath. Ace saw her kick the backs of its knees, causing the colossal cyborg to drop. Kaitlyn let a smirk creep on her lips, but it was quickly replaced with shock as the machine spun its upper body around to face her. It had her by the throat in an instant. It whipped her to the side once more, sending her crashing across the town square.

Kaitlyn was rushing the robot again. Her hair was matted with sweat and blood ran down over her left eye as well as from the corners of her mouth. The machine just walked towards her, throwing a punch at her once again. She pivoted to the side, it's fist grazing her shoulder. It had shattered the bone completely, and now her arm hung limply at her side. However, Kaitlyn did not stop. She dove forward with her hand outstretched to touch it's core. Just as the cyborg used it's other arm to grab her she dropped to the ground on her stomach. Ace saw her demonic grin as the robot's hand was still going with the momentum of the swing and smashed into it's own chest. The machine's eyes immediately turned blue and it stood up straight. Ace, as well as Gabriella, Isabel and Kieron all gawked at the cyborg. Ace saw the robot's core shatter, but it was quickly repaired at an amazing speed. It began to *whir* and *chatter* again as it fixed itself.

"Subject Three has passed the qualification test. Elemental and power restoration permitted." It said in it's gravelly voice. Kaitlyn gasped and soon stood back up. All of her injuries were almost immediately gone. The machine then turned and looked to Ace and Gabriella. *"Any other experiments prepared for the qualification test?"* It asked. Ace made eye contact with Isabel and Kieron before standing firmly in front of Gabriella. He opened his mouth to speak, but his eyes widened when he realized he could not. He was frozen in place, unable to move or speak. His eyes shifted to Isabel and Kieron and saw they were in the same situation. His body was not responding to him as he tried to move, or even make some kind of noise. He couldn't understand what was going on until he made eye contact with Kaitlyn.

No way... there's absolutely no way. Ace thought, narrowing his eyes at the insane girl that stood beside the *HEB*.

Yes way, Kaitlyn's voice echoed in Ace's mind, *I'm sorry that it had to end this way for you... but, at least I haven't broken my promise. You have Arsen's chip. If you really want... I can bring him back with that.*

Ace felt rage build up inside him. He felt his blood boil as he clenched his jaw, shooting her a glare.

"No more testing, *Victorum*. They are not worthy." Kaitlyn told, walking around in front of *Victorum*. The robot only looked down at her. "*Clavis Regni.*" She said in a commanding tone. *Victorum* stood rigid and was silent a moment. Kaitlyn reached out and tapped the circular object in it's chest. The orb came out and a holographic keyboard presented itself. Kaitlyn quickly entered some sort of password before entering her own name. No, it was not her name that she typed out. Ace just managed to glimpse what she had put in the box labeled "name". He felt his breath catch and bit back a forbidden scream. Kaitlyn entered the name and *Victorum chattered* once again before reabsorbing the orb into it's chest. Suddenly, it got down on one knee, head bowed before Kaitlyn.

"Abbadon, *I, as well as my three brothers* Mors, Fames *and* Bellum, *are under your command from now on. What is it that you shall have me do?*"

Made in the USA
Columbia, SC
27 July 2021